Don't Tell

a

Jim Wasowski & Connie Friess

PAGE PUBLISHING, INC.
Conneaut Lake, PA

First originally published by Page Publishing 2020

ISBN 978-1-6624-1693-4 (pbk)
ISBN 978-1-6624-1694-1 (digital)

Printed in the United States of America

Chapter 1

Sitting in the middle seat on an airplane was not Jacob Markowski's idea of fun. Often the guy on his right was obese. Often the woman on his left forgot to wear deodorant when she nervously prepared for her flight. But most often the fellow travelers wanted to talk and expected Jacob to reciprocate. It wasn't that he was not social, but participating in small talk was not his idea of fun. On this trip, however, none of that mattered. Even though the flight from Cleveland to Fort Lauderdale was almost three hours long, Jacob had prepared for it for many years; and nothing could bother him, including fat, smelly folks who loved to talk about boisterous grandkids and the wonders of Japanese rock gardens.

On this trip, he was smart enough to take his lisinopril and atenolol to control his blood pressure, enabling him to stay relaxed enough to tolerate his seatmates and politely listen as Pete explained what he was doing to lose weight and as Rita complimented him on his blue eyes and his nice build for a man of his age! The downside of taking his pills led to making two bathroom trips, which Rita unexpectedly enjoyed as Jacob accidentally braced himself on her ample breasts as he stumbled in the aisle when unexpected turbulence jostled the plane. Jacob blushed while Rita smiled as she began to sweat even more.

*****

Jacob was a baby boomer. His father, Leonard, had served in the big war and was one of those guys who loved to brag that he was a member of the greatest generation. Jacob's mother, Adele, patiently waited for Leonard during the war and often was jealous of his escapades as he traveled to exotic places like Lincoln, Nebraska, Pensacola, Florida, and Shreveport, Louisiana, while being paid by Uncle Sam to be an airplane mechanic. Adele had never left Cleveland and even considered enlisting in the army just to see the world. Instead, she contributed to the war effort by making uniforms, growing gardens to save food for the troops, and working at her local Catholic church to inspire all the downtrodden whose war losses were often too much to bear. When asked if she could wait for the return of her high school sweetheart, Adele would often point to Penelope, the faithful wife of Homer's Odysseus, who waited twenty years for the return of her husband as he fought the Trojan War. "If she can wait twenty years for her husband, I can certainly wait a few years for the return of my true love," she would often say.

Adele's beauty was breathtaking. She had that Lauren Bacall 1940s look that included a pouting smile and a hip toss that drove men wild. The suitors were numerous, but Adele remained true to Leonard despite thinking about giving into temptation, especially when she got his letters describing his escapades at the bars and saloons near his bases.

"Yes, he dances with other women, but he tells me that nobody compares to me, and I think he certainly is someone worth waiting for," Adele once said to her friend Clara who often urged her to get back out there and find another man. "Can't do it, Clara. I know that he loves me. I know that we were meant to be together."

Leonard returned to Cleveland at the end of the war. Adele was waiting with open arms and joked that he looked more like Humphrey Bogart than ever, especially after escalating that smoking habit that now was more than one pack a day. At five feet ten inches and weighing a solid 170 pounds, Leonard was a catch. He had served his nation well not only as a mechanic but as a test pilot who had to fly the planes that he repaired before he sent then back into service across the Pacific. It did not bother her that Leonard's last base was in Hollywood, California, and that he spent almost every night dancing with floozies, celebrities, and lonely women at the bars on the Sunset Strip. All that mattered now was that he was back home, and they could begin their life together.

And so they did. Married at the venerable St. Stanislaus church in front of family, friends, classmates, and even some of the teachers from Cleveland South High School, Leonard and Adele began their married adventure with the promise that they would spend the rest of their lives together. They agreed that they would have a family and that Adele would stay home to raise the kids (two of each sex if they were lucky) while Leonard would be the breadwinner. After all, that was what men were supposed to do back in 1946, and Adele agreed that women must do the most important job, which was to raise their family. He had done his duty. Now she would do hers.

Jacob Andrew Markowski was born in October 1947. His sisters, Dorothy and Peggy, arrived in 1949, and in 1952 and his brother, Richard, arrived in 1957, completing the wish of his parents for two boys and two girls. Leonard got a job at the US Steel Plant in the Cleveland flats and spent his time driving through congested traffic that was complicated by polluted skies that often turned orange. No, the air was not fit to breathe, but for a guy from Leonard's generation, being a man meant that you could overcome anything, especially if you could have a shot or two after work with your buddies in a tavern whose smoke filled malaise was their main contribution to the dirty environment. It didn't matter that the Cuyahoga River was polluted enough to catch on fire someday because men had to be men, and that included at least pretending to be tough. Hell, working near a blast furnace was no big deal for this generation.

Leonard and Adele moved into a small one-bedroom apartment on Sobieski Avenue to begin their lives together. The rent was $35 a month, and that included a refrigerator, a stove, some furniture, and a view overlooking the flats of Cleveland. Living in the Polish neighborhood was almost required by the times. Cleveland, like most big cities, was segregated by ethnic and racial lines. At one point, there were over sixty such neighborhoods in the city, and the lines of demarcation were clear. So, unless you wanted to change your name, options of where to live were limited unless you wanted to bother with the hate, racial, and ethnic strife common in the time. But the neighborhood was true to the values of the Markowski family. In the summertime, accordions could be heard through the open windows as young men tried to become the next Frankie Yankovic. The Cleveland Indians baseball games were heard on every radio in the neighborhood as the locals hoped they could replicate their championship from 1948. Broadcaster Jimmy Dudley became a celebrity because of the team; and if Lou Boudreau, the great Tribe shortstop, or Otto Graham, the great Cleveland Browns' quarterback, was seen in the neighborhood, eyes lit up, autographs were signed, and smiles prevailed.

The smells of fresh Polish sausage were prevalent. Stores popped up to bake the *pączkis* that were baked daily but enjoyed the most on Fat Tuesday, the day before Ash Wednesday, and on Dyngus Day, the day after Easter. Polish was spoken much more than English, especially when the old folks did not want the young kids to understand the conversation, and the feast of the Assumption was the highlight of the summer with parades, great food, and libations in big supply.

Dyngus Day was a wonderful celebratory day where gluttony, debauchery, and drunkenness were finally acceptable after the sacrifices of the Lenten season, where young boys were allowed to use tree branches to tickle the knees of girls that they fancied, and where politicians promised the world to people in return for their votes. If a politician was not a success at the Dyngus Day picnic held at the

Polish Democratic Club, he was never going to win any election even if it was for dogcatcher.

As most women did in the late forties and fifties, Adele worked hard to raise the children, cook great meals on a strict budget, and clean the house. There was little time for chats with friends, long lunches, or taking naps because duty always was calling. But to Adele, raising a great family was the most important thing in the life of a woman. Adele loved her children and would make any sacrifice for them because, like most ethnic American women, she believed in making a lifelong commitment to her family.

By the time Jacob turned four, his name had morphed into "Jake," a name that he used for the rest of his life. In fact, he often forgot that his real name was Jacob when elderly relatives called him that later in life. Three of his grandparents were alive until Jake was in his teens. Leonard's father, Petro, had died of a massive stroke while Leonard was in California during the war. Petro's wife, Stella, loved Jacob but was old before her time and spent most of her time rocking in her rocking chair as she watched the numerous Westerns that engulfed the TV screens of the fifties. She loved *Gunsmoke* the most. Jake never remembered seeing her out of that chair. Adele's parents, Lottie and Felix, lived about a mile from their daughter and often entertained Jake with the snacks that he never got at home in return for his help manicuring their flower beds and gardens. Jake loved the smell of the flowers but loved the pies, cakes, and ice cream she served him even more. It was a great deal for all of them. Felix worked at a tool-and-die plant, never drove a car in his lifetime, and often rode his Schwinn bicycle to Jake's house. He loved it, and the exercise helped him ward off the emphysema that was slowly taking away his health. Jake looked forward to the day when he could ride his own bike to Grandpa's house.

When he reached the age of five, Jake began school at St. Stanislaus, the very church where his parents had married. Being wacked on the knuckles by Sister Leonida and Sister Loyola when he was not sitting up straight made Jake behave in school, but he often wondered if Jesus himself would have condoned such behavior from the good sisters of the Holy Cross Seminary. On Fridays Jake and his classmates were told to put bread wrappers on their feet, tie them on with rubber bands, and then shuffle along the floor to polish it since the wrappers were coated with wax. They couldn't leave for the weekend unless the floor was polished to the satisfaction of the nuns. When Jake searched the Baltimore Catechism for allowable behavior by nuns, using a ruler to torment a kid was never there, and being used as slave labor wasn't either! Later in life Jake undoubtedly remembered these incidents as he considered using violence for a worthy and noble cause.

One day, when Jake was six, his father came home all giddy because he had a big announcement to make. Leonard announced that he had enough money to buy the family its first home! Things were going well for US Steel. The company was benefitting from the Marshall Plan, which was a boon to the rebuilding of Europe, and US Steel got many of the contracts for the steel used to build there. The Korean War was also nearing an end, and restoring South Korea was also going to benefit the US businesses. Times were good, and America found itself as the savior of the world with some unexpected economic benefits for all Americans, especially for large cities like Cleveland, with the population of over one million people and as big as it would ever get. Getting a house and maybe even a new car was a payoff for what Leonard and Adele did during and after the war. The good times for Jake's family had arrived!

Like many families in Cleveland during the 1950s, the Markowskis worked hard, laughed together, cried together, and argued with each other a lot, but always valued the things they were taught at home by their extended families and at school. The family's new house was in West Park on the far-west side of Cleveland. It was a lovely neighborhood near the beautiful metro parks and the Rocky River, with great schools and wonderful restaurants. It was near the Triskett Rapid Transit stop that made a trip to downtown Cleveland take only fifteen minutes. Shopping excursions to Higbee's, The May Company, and Halle's could now be done without waiting for Leonard to drive the family in the Studebaker. Jake wondered when his parents would allow him to take the Rapid downtown on his own. They had great movies in those theatres, but in the meantime, the Riverside Theatre on the corner of Rocky River and Lorain Roads and the Variety on 117th and Lorain were close enough to enjoy since, in this age, television was in its infancy and didn't even go on the air until six o'clock at night. Playing outside after school and going to the movies on Saturdays was nirvana for Jake and his friends.

After he moved his family to the west side of Cleveland, Leonard pulled Jake and Dorothy out of Catholic school and sent them to the local Cleveland schools after reading that the West Park schools were some of the best in the country. The kids loved the fact that their knuckles were only injured in playground skirmishes instead of by nuns with rulers. Jake met many of his longtime friends on those playgrounds and won his share of fights. A shot to the jaw by Ronnie

Kalmar once resulted in Jake getting two stitches in his chin, but Ronnie got five!

The family attended Our Lady of Angels on Sundays, a church that overlooked the park. God never created a more-beautiful setting for folks who wanted to get to know him. Leonard insisted that his children still had to get a Catholic education and made them attend Confraternity of Christian Doctrine classes once a week at the church. At one of those classes, Jake got his knuckles smashed by the Catholic teacher as he had the audacity to ask if people who were in hell because they ate meat on Friday would ever be forgiven and sent to heaven now that Catholics could now become Friday carnivores. Dorothy laughed uncontrollably as she told her parents about the antics of her mischievous brother!

When Jake first saw his new home, he could not believe that he would have his own bedroom and that the new TV antenna could pull in four stations as opposed to the three that the set in their apartment received. Not having to sleep in the same room with one or both of his sisters was also a big thing for a young guy beginning a new life. On Sundays Leonard would drive the family in the 1953 Studebaker to a new place called McDonalds that featured burgers, fries, and shakes for forty-five cents a person. Jake learned to love the Cleveland Indians and hate Willie Mays who robbed Vic Wertz with a great catch in the 1954 World Series. That catch might be the best in baseball history. Jake even tried his hand at pitching when he was ten as he hoped to emulate Herb Score and Early Wynn and Bob Feller—all Tribe legends. He even made his sister Dorothy wear a catcher's mitt as they tossed the ball in their backyard. Yes, they had a backyard! Jake went on to become a particularly good pitcher, making all-star teams and all league teams. He wanted to play professionally until he realized that he wasn't quite good enough when he competed in high school against Steve Stone, a great player who did make it to the major leagues and won a Cy Young Award as the best pitcher in all of baseball.

Jake became a lover of the Cleveland Browns and their quarterback, Otto Graham, and their great receivers like Mac Speedie and Dante Lavelli and relished the great success of the team as he attended their championship parades. When Jim Brown, arguably the greatest football running back ever, visited Jake's school, it was as if God had descended from heaven to bless his flock because to the kids of Cleveland, including Jake, Brown was a god!

*****

Jake was now seventy years of age. He had shrunken to five feet ten inches, was a little overweight, had thinning grey hair, and suffered from the normal aches and pains that come with age. So, as the plane neared the Fort Lauderdale airport, Jake grew more and more uncomfortable with his sandwiched place between his seatmates. Maybe he should have taken a later flight. He tried not to think of the size of Pete on his right or the odor of Rita on his left; although he did enjoy the accidental fondling of her breasts. He instead thought of his childhood. Jim Brown came to mind; the love of his parents came to mind; the values and morals and ethics that he learned in school came to mind; and of course, his old friends came to mind. How in the name of heaven was he ever going to murder the man that changed his life forever? Could he do it? Were his friends really going to help him? What if he gets caught? What if he was wrong about Henry Viper?

Chapter 2

Jake's seatmates got more annoying as the flight seemingly took forever. Pete's large elbows sitting to Jake's right got sharper, and Rita's drunkenness on his other side had reached the point where she was being totally obnoxious. Jake listened politely as Pete tried to explain how he had gained all the weight, and Jake bit his tongue as he really wanted to tell Pete the dangers of obesity.

"It causes cancer, diabetes, heart disease, dumbass," he said to himself.

Rita tried to explain her drinking problem and how she had been amused at the ticket counter in Cleveland as she watched a young man become belligerent when he was told that he would have to pay an extra $50 if he wanted to put his skateboard in his checked bag. Why drunks want to discuss such petty nonsense just didn't matter to Jake anymore. Fort Lauderdale was closer and closer, and he wouldn't have to wait much longer to make Henry Viper pay for his sins.

For the last thirty minutes of the flight, Jake put on his headphones to at least make his seatmates think that he was listening to some music. He wasn't. He was merely thinking about what was bringing him to this point. His mind immediately called up Danielle Simone Stevens. She would be meeting him in Fort Lauderdale and had promised to help him in any way that he needed. Would she really be there for him, or would she chicken out? Did she hate Henry Viper as much as he did? Could they avenge the wrongs that Henry had done?

*****

Jake had met Danielle when they were both entering the sixth grade at Newton D. Baker Middle School. The school got its name from Baker, a native Clevelander, who had served as Secretary of War during World War 1 and spent time as the mayor of Cleveland. At one time in his career, he made a lot of waves by asking restaurants to feed the homeless with the leftover food that they had at the end of the day. Despite the controversy that arose from the idea, it was a given that a Cleveland school would be named for him. At Baker Mrs. Georgina Voll sat Danielle next to Jake in their sixth-grade English class. It did not take long for Jake to notice Danielle. Her long black hair, her long legs, and her blooming breasts were there to see for the entire world, and Jake happily got a great view of all her every day. He often wondered if the other boys in the class noticed the beauty that he saw in her. Danielle was at least bilingual and spoke French often to impress Jake, whose hormones were starting to kick in. To him, there was nothing sexier than a young lady who spoke French! Yes, Jake knew something about sexiness even at his young age.

As the year passed, Jake saw that Danielle was smiling at him more and more, that she was flicking her eyes whenever he gazed at her, and that she was even saying, "Hi, Jake," when he reached his seat. To Jake, all this was meaningful, but he was never sure how to react to any of it. Should he discuss this with his male friends? Would they laugh at him? Was she out of his league? Was he too young to have a girlfriend? Was he misconstruing her gazes and friendliness? Would the school bullies beat him up because he was moving in on a girl that they expected to be theirs since they were often the cool guys?

One of those cool guys, also a bully, was Ron Bloodstone. Ron was big for twelve years of age and walked around school with a white T-shirt, blue jeans, and a well-combed pompadour that had many of the girls thinking he was a young version of James Dean. Ron's dad was in jail, something that Ron was proud of, and he often acted like he, too, would end up in the slammer just like his dad. Ron and Jake had been teammates on their Little League team, and Ron was the star. He hit home runs. He stole bases. He made great catches, and the girls who came to the games loved to watch him play. Jake was the star pitcher on the team and wondered why the girls liked a young slugger like the Cleveland Indians' Rocky Colavito more than they liked a young pitcher like Bob Feller, another great Indians player. Why didn't they root for the pitchers? Once Jake tossed a one-hit shutout, one of his best games ever, but he could not understand why the girls surrounded Ron after the game instead of him, since he had been the big hero for his team.

Just before spring break, near the end of his sixth-grade year, Jake got the courage to ask Danielle if he could carry her books and walk her home. She smiled and said yes. Jake's new best friend, Bruce Goodman, had found out that Danielle lived on Rocky River Drive in a big house overlooking the park. That meant a long walk out of his way, but that didn't matter to Jake, whose West Park home was on a less-elegant, tree-lined street where modest homes were filled with factory workers, teachers, fireman, and policeman. Danielle obviously came from a wealthier family, and as he walked and talked to her, he wondered what it would be like to meet her family. Were they doctors or lawyers or politicians? No matter what they were, Jake wondered what he would say to them and hoped that he could impress them enough to have them accept him if he began hanging around or even dating their lovely daughter.

"Hey, Danielle, how did you like the Big Chuck and Houlihan Show on Friday night? Isn't that Tim Conway a real hoot? Isn't Little John the most acrobatic midget you have ever seen?" Jake said.

Well, maybe it was not the best first line in the history of the world, but when Danielle smiled and said, "I loved it, Jake," Jake thought that he was off to a great start!

None of that mattered though because when Jake and Danielle approached her gigantic home, Ron Bloodstone was standing in front of the house, wearing that white T-shirt and wearing a black leather jacket, looking very much like the rebel that he was pretending to be.

"Hi, Danielle," he said, "my, you are looking good today."

Danielle smiled, and Jake ran away.

Jake was embarrassed. He felt humiliated. He felt sick to his stomach. How could Danielle do this to him? Maybe she didn't like his big nose. Maybe she hates Big Chuck and Houlihan. As he ran home, half sobbing but trying not to wail out loud, Jake saw Bruce Goodman riding his bike along Warren Road near the new rib joint that was opening in the Warren Village Shopping Center. Jake sprinted toward Bruce and almost knocked him off his bike as he forced him to stop.

"What's wrong, buddy? How'd it go with Danielle? Did you hold her hand? Did she let you in her house? Did she invite you to her room?"

Bruce was talking in a voice that had not quite reached puberty, and he was sounding like a young robin learning how to chirp.

Jake slowly calmed down and explained what happened.

"I'm never going to talk to a girl again," Jake said with a tinge of sadness in his voice.

Bruce, acting like a true friend, was supportive.

"Jake, maybe she didn't know that Ron would be there. Maybe he just showed up and was jealous that she was walking with you. And remember, Jake, that she chose you to walk her home, not him."

Bruce's words seemed to calm Jake down. As he walked home that night, he was glad that spring break was about to start and that he wouldn't have to see Danielle for another week. What he would say to her when he did see her was now the big question in his life.

Jake spent his spring break tossing baseballs, playing street football, and running through the metro parks. The hill down Detroit Road into the park was a challenge even for the most-fit athlete, but Jake rode his bike up and down the hill in order to get into great physical shape not only for his baseball season but to also urge his body to start developing size and muscle, something that seemed to be delayed in his life. What did Ron Bloodstone have over him other than huge size for a sixth grader and an attitude of being a rebel? Why are cute girls attracted to guys like him? The bike rides also reduced the stress that all this had created for him. Leonard and Adele sensed that something was different about Jake but did not push when he refused to talk about it. Jake loved to watch the TV show, *Leave It to Beaver,* and often wondered how his life might be different if Ward and June were his parents. But he also learned quickly that real-life problems are not fixed in the time span of a thirty-minute TV show. He loved his parents and knew that they would always be there for him no matter what. That thought alone served to comfort him as he was going through his first coming-of-age crisis.

On the Monday after spring break, Jake was the last one to enter his English class. He did not get seated until after the tardy bell rang. Mrs. Voll gave him a stern look and reminded him that he must be on time. Danielle was seated next to him and was staring straight ahead. She took her spelling test, diagrammed a few sentences, and never once looked at Jake nor spoke to him.

But at the end of class, she rose to leave, looked at Jake, and said, "I'm sorry."

Jake was stunned. Was she apologizing to him? He could not believe it. As they walked down the hall together, Danielle confessed that she had used Jake to catch Ron's eye. She didn't know why she was attracted to a rebel like Ron and didn't know if she was really attracted to him at all. She was as confused as anyone and wanted to be friends with Jake.

"Friends?" she said quietly to him.

"Friends," Jake replied. "What exactly does that mean? Would we hang out together? Would we talk on the phone? What exactly do you mean?"

Danielle didn't know how to answer him. Instead she smiled, gave Jake a peck on his cheek, and simply said, "Jake, I think you're a great guy, and I really do like you a lot." Then she walked down the long hallway to her next class.

One of the traditions at Baker Middle School was the end-of-the-year dance. All the sixth, seventh, and eighth graders were invited

JIM WASOWSKI & CONNIE FRIESS

to attend. The school's gym teachers and shop teachers volunteered to spin the tunes of the day and chaperone the students. Unlike St. Stanislaus, Jake's first school, Baker teachers didn't go around separating young couples on the dance floor if they were too close to each other, and yes, some of the couples did get awfully close. Bruce asked Jake if he was going to the dance.

Jake, who was just starting to get over his crush on Danielle, said, "Why not? Let's do it. Maybe we'll get ourselves one of those older eighth-grade girls!"

"Heck," said Bruce, "we wouldn't know what to do even if we got to dance with one of them."

They smiled as they both were enjoying the ridiculousness of ever even imagining the possibility of luring those eighth graders!

Back in the fifties, middle-school dances presented a chance to fulfill the dreams of every prepubescent kid in the country. First, the boy didn't have to ask the girl out, which was the hardest thing to do. Second, all the potential girls were there in one place at one time. And third, if you asked them to dance, it was proper for them to say yes because if they said no, a gigantic scene would be sure to happen. And nobody wanted that. Boys were separated into one area of the bleachers, and girls were placed in another section. At the end of each song, the dancers had to return to their seats as everyone awaited the announcement of whether the next song was going to be a gentlemen's or ladies' choice. For the Baker students, it was great to be called gentlemen and ladies at such an early stage of their lives. All the kids sucked on breath mints or chewed gum because they knew the value of proper smelling, minty breath when they were dancing, and many even underwent Clearasil treatments for weeks before the dance to ward off their unwanted zits. There were also rumors that some of those wild eighth-grade girls were wearing falsies to lure the more-mature boys. When Jake and Bruce heard that news, they weren't exactly sure what it meant, but both Paul Handley and Pat Torrence, the stars of the football team, said that, for sure, those falsies will give you a boner. That sounded exciting to both Jake and Bruce.

Teachers George Urbanski and Clem Downer were the DJs for the Baker dances. Urbanski taught science and sex ed during the day and was the football coach after school and DJ at the dances. Downer was the shop teacher during the day and the basketball coach in the winter and another one of the DJs at the dances. They were in their early thirties, but most of the Baker students perceived them as old folks who did not understand any of the whims and fads of the day.

Still, though, they were there for the kids, and the kids appreciated what they were doing. Jake especially had an affinity for Downer even though every time Jake tried to make an elaborate piece of furniture in shop class under his wonderful guidance, the piece always turned into a cutting board!

Mr. Downer, announced it was a ladies' choice. The song was *It's Late* by Ricky Nelson. Both Jake and Bruce looked at each other and acknowledged that their ability to dance to a fast song was equal to that of a turtle running across the road. It did not exist. Most of the boys also refused to dance as well, and the floor was only filled with eighth-grade boys who were too tough to be told by anyone that they couldn't dance. Their partners were often girls who spent some of the night hiding in the restroom, smoking a cigarette in hopes that they would not be found by Mrs. Voll who preferred teaching English to busting the girls who were trying to be mature beyond their years.

After five fast songs, Mr. Downer announced it a ladies' choice. The song was going to be *Mr. Blue* by The Fleetwoods. Suddenly every boy sprinted back to his seat in the gym, and the restrooms emptied. Every male student at Baker Middle School sat there and wondered which girl, if any, would ask them to dance. Danielle was one of the first girls up as she asked Ron Bloodstone to be her partner. He was dressed in his normal garb and looked more muscular than ever. Then Barbara Moody, perhaps the most intelligent girl in the sixth grade, got up and asked Bruce Goodman to dance. He blushed to a degree that made his face redder than his hair, something that added to his overall gawkiness, but then smiled as Jake punched him lightly in the arm to congratulate him. Bruce seemingly was in heaven. And then it happened. As Jake was congratulating Bruce, Michelle Navarre came up to Jake and asked him to dance.

Jake smiled and said, "Of course."

As the night continued, Bruce and Barbara and Jake and Michelle danced every slow dance together, held each other tight, and had the best night of their young lives.

*****

As Jake's plane taxied to the gate in Fort Lauderdale, his mind was spinning in many directions. Would Danielle, Bruce, Ron, and Barbara all arrive in time to board the cruise ship that Henry Viper would also be boarding? Danielle was flying in from Los Angeles, Bruce from Indianapolis, Ron from Cleveland, and Barbara from

Houston. They had all gone their separate ways after high school, but Jake and Barbara felt that what Henry Viper had done during their younger days needed a reconciliation. They all had successful careers, now retired, and knew that they were closer to the end of their lives than the beginning. On this cruise, Jake worried about nothing other than getting back at Henry Viper. He wondered if on this cruise, would they all agree to get back at Henry?

Chapter 3

Jake took a cab to the Fort Lauderdale cruise terminal to board Royal Caribbean's *Allure*, one of the biggest cruise ships in the world. His mind continued to think about his reunion with his old friends, Danielle, Bruce, Ron, and Barbara. He had not seen all of them together since their high school graduation party, and that night was nothing more than a blur.

*****

Danielle, Bruce, Barbara, Michelle, and Jake had become the best of friends as they finished their final two years at Baker and went on to John Marshall High School on W. 140th Street. Ron was still a rebel and never much part of Jake's circle of friends. Marshall had the reputation, deservedly so, of being the best high school in Cleveland. In 1959 author James Conant, the one-time president of Harvard University, wrote a book called *The American High School Today*. The book cited the school as being one of the best schools in the country and certainly the best in Cleveland. Marshall's reputation grew and was a reason for people to move to the west side of Cleveland.

The school blossomed in the sixties and grew to over four thousand students, making its student body way too large for its gothic-looking towers. It's gigantic smokestack and towers themselves were in the landing pattern of nearby Cleveland Hopkins Airport, with planes flying over the building once or even twice every minute. The resulting noise combined with the enthusiasm of so many young adults made W. 140th one of the noisiest streets in the country. The conditions were rectified by grouping students into shifts so that some started class at 7:30 in the morning, and others started at 9:00. That was the only way that the administration could fit the students into the limited number of classrooms. Jake, Michelle, and Bruce were chosen to begin class on the early shift while Danielle, Ron, and Barbara were on the late shift.

Luckily for Jake, Michelle was also assigned to the early shift, which made it possible for him and Michelle to walk to school together under the influence of the darkness and gloom prevalent in Cleveland at 7:00 a.m. most of the school year. Hand-holding and cuddling were easily accomplished in the darkness. They had walked to Baker for their final two years at the school and were the cutest couple in the building. Michelle had grown into a petite young lady with a well-proportioned body, a beautiful smile that featured a come-hither look, and a haircut that made her look like actress Natalie Wood. She had short black hair that featured bangs dropping almost to her eyebrows. When she entered college after her later separation from Jake, he saw a picture of her and noticed that her hair had grown longer and was almost to her waist, but she still had those beautiful bangs, along with the look of a flower child. Jake loved that picture.

As luck would have it, Jake and Michelle started their school day in Room 306 on the first day of high school in 1961. Their homeroom teacher, who they would share for four years, was Jim Thomas. His job was to counsel the new kids, read them the daily announcements, and enlighten them about the history of JMH. If he could create some school spirit along the way, that, too, was fine. When Jake found out that Mr. Thomas was also one of the baseball coaches, he lit up even more because Jake continued to excel as a player, especially as a pitcher, and was hoping that Mr. Thomas could give him some advice on how to make the baseball team. Jake had grown four inches since his days in sixth grade. At five feet nine inches and 145 pounds, he was no longer one of the smaller kids in class. Paul Handley, one of the pitchers on the team who was thought to be much better than Jake during their middle-school years, even complimented Jake on his growth spurt but then followed the nice words with a rough "nuggie" on the back of Jake's head. Paul, who had been the big man on campus in middle school, liked to do that a lot. Jake kept hoping that the day would come soon for this youthful form of torture and bullying to stop. Not only did the nuggie really hurt, but Paul really had big knuckles, which served to exasperate the pain even more. Jake hoped that maybe a big senior guy would give Paul a nuggie. In fact, Jake often thought of paying a senior to get his revenge on Paul.

Bruce and Barbara also continued as a couple throughout high school; although Barbara, who became the senior-class valedictorian, often preferred studying, cutting up frogs, working as a candy striper, and running every club at JMH to going out with Bruce. Bruce thus had a wandering eye, and with maybe two thousand girls to look at every single day, it was easy to get distracted, especially when Barbara was running the French club rather than smooching with him in the back row of the Variety Theatre. Barbara was tall, long-legged, and well-proportioned but chose to hide her figure by wearing a baggy dress to school or a frocked coat when she was working in her labs. She didn't want too many guys to notice her. Her agenda was to get out of school and then make her mark in the world as a doctor. Having a serious boyfriend was not part of her plan.

Barbara loved Jerry Klaybor, her biology teacher, and served as his teacher assistant for her junior and senior years. She not only graded his quizzes but helped many squeamish students dissect their frogs, helped them study their grasshoppers under an electron microscope, and even chaperoned the students on a field trip to the medical examiner's office where they hoped to see a dead body or two. Looking into a microscope was something that Barbara relished despite the protests of Bruce, who still had that wandering eye.

When John F. Kennedy was assassinated in November 1963, Barbara was in her chemistry class, leading the class in a titration experiment. She was using Bruce as her foil, and the class was eating up every bit of the fun. The principal, John Cihlar, a lifeless man who resembled Lurch from *The Addams Family* TV show, came on the public address system and announced that the president had been shot and died. The shock of the moment led to silence by most, tears from some, and painful expressions by many. The teacher, Clarence Murphy, expressed his horror at the event and escorted the kids out of the room as they were told to leave early for the day. When the news came, Barbara collapsed into Bruce's arms, her eyes filled with tears, and she sobbed until it hurt. Bruce knew at that point that Barbara was special, and he wanted to hold onto her forever.

Danielle continued to see Ron Bloodstone, but the scuttle-butt was that Ron was following the crime-filled ways of his father. When they were juniors, Danielle confessed to Jake and Bruce that she thought Ron might have stolen a car. Later that school year she thought that he had robbed a drunk at a bar on the corner of Rocky River and Lorain Roads and was also concerned that he was seeing other girls behind her back. Ron had grown up physically and was now six feet two inches and 180 pounds. Danielle had resisted his sexual approaches for several years and feared that he would force himself on her. If that happened, she had no idea how she would respond or what she would do. Danielle seemed to age as her high school years progressed. The aging was not flattering, and by the time high school graduation arrived, she looked like she had been taken through the ringer because Ron had abused her in every way you could imagine. Danielle never told anyone about this abuse and spent many nights crying herself to sleep as the problem worsened.

For the most part, high school was fun for Jake, Bruce, Barb, and Michelle. They went to games together, hit Bob's Big Boy after the games to celebrate a victory or the losses, and enjoyed the winter formals, even though the guys still could not dance. They went to the movies together, but totally ignored the show, and developed friendships with each other that they thought would last for a lifetime, if those friendships didn't grow into something more.

They were great students. Jake loved history and fell in love with the humor that John Darbowski used to teach his world-history classes. In fact, Jake once told Mr. Darbowski that he should get a part-time job as a stand-up comic. Jake decided early on that being a history teacher might be something that he would like to pursue if he could be like Mr. Darbowski, who once humored his class when he described the pyramids of Cheops as "being built by a pharaoh, Cheops, who desired to have the biggest erection in the history of the world!" Yes, the boys all roared, and the girls blushed, and even Darbowski could not stop laughing.

Michelle loved languages. She became the vice president of the French club and the president of the Spanish club. She was a rarity because she took four years of two languages, something that wasn't normally done in high school. She hoped to work at the United

Nations or in foreign service, but it was obvious that she would eventually leave Cleveland to seek out her place in the world.

Bruce and Barbara were often not in the same classes, as his track toward graduation leaned toward business classes while hers was science. Bruce wanted to either be a businessman or a musician. Bruce's father owned a local supply distribution center that sold building items to local contractors, and Bruce knew that he could work for his father if he wanted to. So he enrolled in many of the JMH business classes but found most of them boring and unstimulating. Working with numbers was fine, but he really enjoyed the creative process more and hoped to be a musician. As a member of the choir, he sang baritone; and as a member of the school orchestra and marching band, he played a mean saxophone. Bruce loved that Barbara was also in the band, playing the sousaphone with a group of girls that were known as the Oompa Dolls. The idea of having young ladies play sousaphones was a creation of Omar Whiteman, the band director.

The JMH band was one of the best in Ohio and was so good Whiteman was honored when he became the director of the Ohio State Fair High School Band. When The Beatles hit the world in 1964, Bruce, like most kids, loved them but always thought that they would be a lot better if they had a saxophone leading the rhythm section, and yes, he wanted to be in that band, playing that sax. Ironically, when he was in college at Purdue, Bruce became the social chairman of his fraternity. When he was given the task of hiring a band for a weekend party, he hired an unknown band with a great horn-rhythm section named Chicago Transit Authority or CTA. That band ultimately changed its name to Chicago and did all right! Yes, Bruce knew a lot about music.

Danielle loved to paint. She loved taking her art classes and was wealthy enough to afford many trips to the Cleveland Museum of Art for private classes. Her teachers at JMH usually left her alone because they realized that she had more talent than they did even when they had no idea what she was doing or trying to do. Ron often laughed at her paintings. "What the hell is that thing supposed to be?" was a refrain that he used almost every time she showed him a new piece of work. The closed-mindedness that he displayed became so numbing to her by her senior year she refused to show him her work. That served to make him angrier than he normally was and frightened Danielle even more as she continued to fear the abuse that she almost always expected from Ron. Despite her attractiveness, which was substantial, as she aged, she grew a lot to look like

Mary Travers of Peter, Paul and Mary. In high school Danielle never dated anyone other than Ron and never really acknowledged to anyone that they were a couple. Most just noticed that they were always together and that Danielle never looked happy.

What they did on those dates was not the norm for the times. Yes, he was handsome in a rebellious sort of way, but she often asked herself why she wasn't physically attracted to him. Why didn't she want to get closer to him? And very often she feared what might happen if she tried to break up with him.

Ron Bloodstone and Henry Viper met each other on the streets of Cleveland as they were both cutting class while ninth-grade students at Marshall. They were barely making the grade, and both relayed the message that they were bad asses and loved playing the role. Henry's uncle, Johnny Viper was the local mob boss in town. When Henry wanted something, most times Uncle Johnny got it for him. When his uncle couldn't help him, Henry would just take what he wanted. Even Paul Handley never had the courage to say anything to Ron or Henry when he passed them in the school halls, let alone considered giving them a nuggie. Paul, the big man on campus, was not merely afraid of these guys; he avoided them. Everybody else in the school was traumatized when those two guys came anywhere near them.

When the students at JMH felt that Ron and Henry had gone too far with their intimidation and their threats of violence, some went to the assistant principal to tell him about the violent, criminal behavior and to ask him to reprimand the boys. The head assistant principal, a man named John Pitts, always responded by calling Ron and Henry to the office to give them a "talking to" that resulted in nothing more than more threats and attacks on the other students immediately after the reprimand had ended. John Pitts did not have the ability to discipline anyone. He was five feet four inches, obese with a protruding belly, and had a ruddy complexion that led to screams of "wino" when he chased kids down the hall. No, he couldn't run extremely far, and no, he never caught a kid that he was chasing. To many JMH students, the best senior prank ever was having a greased pig set loose in the halls of JMH and then howling as Mr. Pitts ran down the hall, trying to tackle the slippery bovine! Even the teachers were laughing as they watched the spectacle.

Ron and Henry entered the world of crime when they were both sophomores at JMH. They broke into cars. They robbed drunks on the street. They sold marijuana to middle-school kids. They collected protection money from the immigrant shop owners on Lorain Avenue and gave the money to Henry's Uncle Johnny who in return gave them a nice cut of the take.

Johnny Viper had entered the world of organized crime when he was fourteen. Connected to the roving gangs of Murray Hill in the Mayfield Road area of Cleveland, Johnny began his life of crime by collecting protection money, beating up enemies of his family, and tormenting all that he could. He often felt guilty about many things that he did but alleviated that guilt on Sundays at Holy Rosary Parish by giving a nice tithe of 10 percent to the church. When Henry was born to Johnny's brother, Silvio, Johnny hoped that he and his nephew were very much alike.

Ron was still dating Danielle, but with Henry's help, he finally lost his virginity to one of Uncle Johnny's ladies of the evening who worked out of a beautiful home overlooking Fairview Park. The clients at the house included judges, policemen, firemen, politicians, lawyers, and successful businessmen who would often acknowledge each other with a smile and a wink as they left the building. Henry was the lookout. When Ron climaxed with a real woman for the first time, he yelled out Danielle's name several times. Rita, the real receiver of Ron's seeds, could have cared less!

Ron never understood why Danielle was rejecting him. As he entered his final two years of school, just barely because of his continually horrendous grades, he decided to clean up his act. Maybe being the good boy instead of the bad boy would be a way to enchant Danielle. With his new, illegally gained wealth, he had bought a newer car and started to wear shirts with collars and buttons and tried harder in class to get better grades. He still bragged about his many sexual conquests, which, in truth, were very few, but he still wanted Danielle more than ever.

One night, during their junior year, Ron ran into Jake, Michelle, Barbara, and Bruce at Tony's Diner, a popular restaurant at Kamm's Corners on Rocky River and Lorain. The diner was a hangout for west-siders for over fifty years and was often frequented by Jake and Sarah, his eventual wife, when they were both teachers at JMH. Ron walked up to the group whom he had tormented for years and politely asked if he could join them. You never said no to Ron, so they agreed but answered with suspicion and trepidation. Ron was being civil to them for one of the first times in his life. He apologized for some of his antics and blamed all that on immaturity. He didn't tell them about his gangster activities but instead asked them for some advice on how to get Danielle to like him.

Bruce answered first and said, "Just be nice to her, Ron. Tell her how you feel about her. Tell her how attractive she is."

Jake added, "Open doors for her, write her wonderful letters, and send her love notes through her girlfriends."

Barbara added, "Be nice and compliment her paintings. Mention how much fun you have with her. Saying that would really help."

Michelle chimed in by saying, "Ron, what you need to consider is that you've really done something to push her away. So come out and directly ask her what you did to offend her. Until you know what's bothering her, you won't be able to get her back."

Ron listened attentively for one of the first times in his life. He was a high school junior, and perhaps he was finally growing up. Yes, Henry had lured him into a dangerous world that gave him money and some status, but for a rare moment, Ron wondered if maybe giving up that status was worth winning over Danielle. Perhaps he should change his ways.

When he discussed his dilemma with Henry, Ron was shocked when he said, "Well, Ron, I have a way to help you out. I've decided to run for senior-class president, and I want you to be my vice president. I bet Danielle will really be impressed when we win." Ron was shocked by the announcement. How in the hell could the two gang-sters win any type of election?

After Michelle and Barbara returned home from Tony's Diner, they did what teenage girls tended to do in the sixties. They went to their phone and called Danielle. They told her about the change in Ron and what advice they had given him.

"Danielle," said Michelle, "he seemed sincere. He seemed remorseful. He seemed like he really wants to be with you. Maybe you should give him another chance."

Barbara put her ear to the phone and said, "What do you have to lose? I've seen a real change in his personality and have seen him pay more attention in class as well as show up on time. That's never happened before. It's all because he wants to win you over, Danielle. Think about it."

Michelle and Barbara ended the call, thinking that they had given Danielle some good advice. Little did they know, it would lead to tragedy. When Danielle hung up the phone, she asked herself if she should throw herself at Ron to acknowledge his change or if she should continue to treat him like the ogre she suspected he really was. She never knew exactly what Ron was doing at night, but she was sure that it was bad because she knew that he hung around with

Henry Viper. When Danielle asked Ron how he got money to buy a new car, Ron made up a completely implausible excuse. When she asked how he had the money to ask her out to extravagant restaurants and concerts, she knew by his shoulder shrug that something wasn't quite right. But what bothered her the most was that other guys were not paying attention to her. Why weren't they asking her out? Were they assuming that she and Ron were a serious item? Did they fear what Ron would do to them if they asked her out? Or was she sending out vibes that said that she was not available to any other guy out there? That possibility worried Danielle a lot.

*****

As Jake's shuttle bus from the airport approached the *Allure* in Fort Lauderdale's beautiful port, all the things that had happened to him in his life kept rolling through his mind like an old black-and-white silent movie. Yes, there was a lot of good. Yes, there had been some bad. And now he knew there was going to be some ugly. What happened to Michelle had traumatized Jake for forty years. Would his friends help him even the score by killing Henry Viper if he could convince them that he had figured out a way to commit the perfect crime? After all, Henry really deserved it, and sometimes becoming a vigilante is the only thing you can do.

Chapter 4

Boarding the *Allure* was easy for Jake. Because he had taken multiple cruises on Royal Caribbean ships, he knew the shortcuts, the routine, and the procedures to board the large ship quickly. He had learned all that from his ex-wife, Sarah, who had worked hard to convince him that cruising on a big cruise ship was much different from the horrid experiences that he had on his chartered fishing trips while vacationing in Florida. On one such trip, off the coast of Fort Myers, Jake and over twenty other fishermen vomited so much from the high seas even the captain considered pursuing another occupation, as the sight and smell was beyond disgusting. Jake was prepared for this trip not only with Dramamine but also with the prescription patch for seasickness, as Sarah had always encouraged him to pack.

Jake took the glass elevator to deck 5 to the Rising Tides, one of the numerous bars on the *Allure*. The ship seemingly had more bars than one could ever visit on a single cruise. There were about fifteen of them that sold wine and liquor. There were also private bars for the Diamond Club members like Jake and private rooms for Diamond Plus members and luxurious lounges for the Pinnacle members. Each of these statuses was attained by the number of cruise days you accumulated. It was almost as if privileged folks had their own wait staff who catered to their every whim. But the Rising Tides was his favorite place on the ship and his choice for this meeting with his friends.

The bar slowly moved from the fifth to the eighth deck of the massive ship. Jake ordered a Manhattan and hoped that he was not too drunk when Bruce, Barbara, Ron, and Danielle finally arrived. They had a lot of business to discuss.

*****

Ron somehow made to the spring of his junior year of high school. He had been suspended ten times. He had more tardiness than any kid in John Marshall history but still managed to get all Ds and an occasional C in his classes. Most of the kids thought that the teachers were passing him just to get him out of the building, knowing that he would never want to drop out because of Danielle. The sexual frustration that he felt was driving him crazy. Near the end of his junior year, Ron's thoughts turned more to what he might do with the rest of his life. He knew he had no skills unless you counted grand larceny. He knew that going to college was something that he would never do, and he knew that his genes were probably going to lead him to something bad or subversive. His father was in jail. His mother, who was only thirty-two, had given up on him and was screwing every guy on the west side of Cleveland.

The election for senior-class officers was held near the end of school year for the juniors so that the new officers could meet in the summer months to make plans for the year ahead. When math teacher, Tom Joniak, also the teacher sponsor of the JMH senior class, found out that Henry Viper and Ron Bloodstone were running as a ticket for the class presidency and vice presidency, he almost resigned.

"Isn't there some sort of rule that I can enact to keep them off the ballot?" he asked Principal John Cihlar.

Cihlar, as stone-faced as always, said, "Not that I know of. We are trying to teach the kids the electoral process, and anyone should be allowed to run just like they can for most political offices. Hell, Harry Truman never went to college, worked at a store that sold hats, and guess what? He turned out to be a great president. So let them run, Tom. I trust our kids enough that they won't vote for them anyway."

Tom Joniak didn't like the answer at all, but he really had no choice.

Marikka Ryan was also running for the presidency and was expected to win easily. She was a brilliant student and a talented athlete, even though she could never display it in the days before Title IX, which finally allowed more competitive opportunities for young women. She was also an aspiring thespian. Her vice-presidential choice was Bobby Kerr. Bobby was the star of the basketball team, a member of the chess team, and planned to go to Harvard. But Bobby was an African American, and nobody was sure if a school that was 98 percent white would vote for a black kid even if he was a great athlete.

Joniak assumed that Viper and Bloodstone would never win, so he encouraged the candidates to campaign hard but fairly. He also remembered that the JMH class of 1961 had voted for Eunice Washburne as their homecoming queen. Eunice was almost three hundred pounds and could not fit into any dress available in a regular-clothes store. Baths and deodorant were usually not a part of her life, and friends were nonexistent. The voters launched a great plot to have everyone write in her name for the homecoming queen. As the votes were counted, and Joniak saw the cruel thing that the students had done, he was appalled. When he announced that the girl who got the second most votes was the winner, the students booed him off the stage because they knew that their votes were not being counted. High school kids can often be cruel, and sometimes their jokes go way too far. When Eunice found out what had happened, she ran away from the homecoming dance in total humiliation. Joniak thus knew that with the names of Viper and Bloodworth on this year's senior-class ballot that if they won, he would have to acknowledge the victory and try to work with them for the next school year as the senior-class advisor. He hated the thought.

When Danielle found out that Ron was running for office, she was befuddled. Maybe he was turning over a new leaf, she thought, or maybe he was really doing this to impress her. But when she saw Ron campaign, give some good speeches, and dress himself well, she was thoroughly impressed. Ron had even gotten his hair cut! It helped a lot that Viper's Uncle John was interested in having the boys win as well. During the campaign, he drove Henry to school in his big limo and enjoyed the moment as students gathered to watch Henry leave the car dressed in a fashionable coat and tie. Uncle Johnny printed campaign signs for Henry and Ron to use that promised things like more dances, more time between classes, better food in the cafeteria, and student disciplinary boards to handle unruly students. Henry and Ron became politicians overnight as they learned the skill of promising everything to every group you talked to, knowing that the reality was that you could likely never fulfill any of your promises if you won.

On the day before the election, a senior-class assembly was held. The presidential candidates, Marikka and Henry, were given ten minutes each to tell their classmates why they should earn their support. Marikka gave a thoughtful, marvelous speech while Henry's words still included wild promises that could never be met. Unfortunately for Marikka, Henry won the election with ease. Rumor had it that Uncle John and Henry and Ron were handing out ten-dollar bills to each junior at JMH to entice them. No words were mentioned other than to be sure to remember where the money came from. The teachers were oblivious to the stunt, and the students treasured the ten dollars, knowing that would buy them two tickets to The Beatles concert about to held at Public Hall in Cleveland. The kids did not realize it, but Uncle Johnny knew that this stunt would clinch the election for his nephew. Still, though, Henry had given a rousing speech that surprised not only the kids but even most of the staff. Maybe there was something redeeming in Henry after all. The kids had no way of knowing that all his promises were empty.

The senior year for Jake, Michelle, Barbara, Bruce, and Danielle went by quickly. College applications were made, part-time jobs were secured, championships were won, books were read mainly by using CliffsNotes, vacations were taken, teenage scandals led to gossip sessions, and friendships were seemingly secured for life. Jake was going off to Indiana University to become a history teacher. Bruce was off to Purdue to learn industrial management. Barbara was going to Ohio State to enter a premed program. Michelle was off to Carnegie Mellon to see if she could perfect five more languages to become an international translator. Danielle, though, had no plans. Her parents pushed her hard and let her know that her family, a family of wealth and prominence, would be embarrassed if she did not go to college. Danielle still painted. Often Ron did not understand her work at all and still made fun of it much like he did when they first met. Was Ron ever going to grow up? After the election, he reverted to dressing as a gangster and a malcontent, and his grades began to slip again. So the turnaround in Ron that Danielle saw during the election was now viewed as a mere ploy to get Danielle into bed. And the more

Danielle rejected Ron, the madder he got. She wanted to love him but not in the way he wanted. She wanted to love somebody. Wasn't that supposed to happen between an eighteen-year-old girl and her boyfriend? What was wrong with her?

The senior prom was the most important, most grandiose event that most of the class would enjoy in their high school days. Guys who had never dated asked girls without a boyfriend to the big event, hoping they would finally have a date. Couples that had been together for weeks or even years planned prom night for ages and hoped to save enough money to rent a limo and have a wonderful dress or tuxedo that made them look sexy or handsome. That list included Jake, Michelle, Barbara, and Bruce, but not Danielle and Ron.

About a month before the prom, Danielle and Ron had a major fight that was much more serious than the same old quarrels that they always had. Ron did not want to take her to the prom. In 1965 it was still every girl's dream to be swept off her feet by a handsome, young man and taken to the biggest dance in their high school years. Yes, Danielle was wondering why she was still with Ron and why she wasn't attracted to him. But girls were expected to go to the prom. Her friends would talk if she did not go. Ron said that he would not be seen dressed up nor would he act respectably toward adults he hated, and after all, he had a bad-boy image to support.

"But Ron, there'll only be one senior prom in our lives. I think you'll regret it later in your life if you don't go," Danielle said in her most-convincing voice.

"Screw that, Danielle. I can barely tolerate this school, and I cannot stand the teachers and most of the people in it. I would not stay in school if you weren't here. I would have dropped out already," Ron protested loudly.

"But Ron, you are the senior-class vice president. Shouldn't you go just because it's expected?"

"Bullshit, Danielle. When have you ever known me to do what was expected? That's not how I roll," yelled Ron with a threatening voice.

After more nasty words were exchanged on both ends, Ron lost complete control of his fractured emotions and pushed Danielle. Then he slapped her in the face as hard as he had ever hit anyone during his numerous fights on the streets. He did it with a look of hate in his eyes.

As he pummeled her, he yelled, "You bitch, nobody tells me what to do. Ever!"

Ron ran as fast as he could and jumped into his GTO, a muscle car that many thought he had stolen. Danielle was in tears. He had never hit her before, even though she often expected him to. She was hurting and didn't know what to do.

As Ron got home and pulled into his driveway, he noticed that a large limousine was parked in front of his house. Henry Viper was driving the large Mercedes Benz, acting like he was a mafioso chauffeur. His longtime pal, Frankie Torino, was also in the car. Frankie supplied the muscle for Uncle Johnny, and he and Henry were not only coworkers but also rivals in the organization. They had always been bigger, stronger, and tougher than Ron; and although they had become comrades in crime, Ron was intimidated by them, and if the truth be told, he was often afraid of them.

"Hey, Henry, what's going on? Why are you guys at my house?" said Ron with a fearful voice.

"I'm here waiting for your mom to finish with my uncle Johnny," Henry said without any consideration for the effects of his words. Ron didn't know what to say. He looked at Henry with a perplexed face. Uncle John came out of the house while still buckling his pants.

As Ron stood there, watching Henry's uncle walk back to his car, knowing what Johnny had just been doing with his mother, his face reddened.

He looked at Henry, who was behind the wheel of the limo, and screamed, "What in the hell are you doing? Are you pimping my mother out to your uncle? Is she one of his women? What's wrong with you?"

Uncle John smiled at Ron and said, "Calm down, son. Your mom's a great lay. You ought to be proud of that, and you know what else? Henry will tell you the same thing. In fact, he recommended her. She really is the best!"

Ron looked back at his house and saw his mother with barely any clothes on, standing in the doorway, smoking a cigarette, and looking at him with a smile. As the limo pulled away, John and Henry were laughing as hard as human beings could laugh. Ron ran down the street in pain. It was not a good way to end the day.

*****

The Rising Tides made great Manhattans, and Jake was enjoying every single one of them. He kept looking at the elevator, hoping that his friends would be on the next one. They had all texted him, alerting him of their arrivals; but when they weren't there yet, he began to question himself, wondering if they were going to show up at all. He wondered if what he was asking of them was right thing to do. And then he decided that this was the stupidest goddamn idea that he had ever thought of.

Chapter 5

Danielle arrived on the *Allure* two hours before the ship was sched-
uled to depart. The airport shuttle carrying Ron, Bruce, and Barbara
got there minutes later. Their flights had been uneventful, which
gave them plenty of time to contemplate what they planned to do on
this trip. They had come from Los Angeles, Cleveland, Indianapolis,
and Houston to join Jake. As they travelled, they each wondered if
they could follow through with what Jake might ask them to do.
They did not know exactly what that might entail, but they all knew
that this trip was extremely important to Jake and Barb. Since their
planes had arrived almost simultaneously, they had agreed to meet at
Chili's Too restaurant in terminal three so they could share a shuttle
to the *Allure*.

As she hugged her high school friends, Danielle seemed nervous, as if she wanted to unburden herself from some untold truth.
Danielle was still petite, feisty, and had the look of the flower child
that she was in high school. She was a hippie before the term became

popular. She looked great in paisley and shyly admitted that she was still painting and that several of her paintings were now on display in the modern-art wing of the Cleveland Museum of Art with her current exhibit in Los Angeles getting rave reviews in the art section of the *Los Angeles Times*. Danielle never went to college. Instead, she left her home after high school to move to Ohio City, a Cleveland neighborhood on the near West Side that was in disarray and depressed at that time in 1965. Danielle worked at many part-time jobs—from bartending to selling clothes at the May Company, a job where she excelled because of her excellent knowledge of styles, fabrics, and design. Her parents couldn't understand her decision but supported her financially when she needed it and emotionally always supported her. When they both died in 1976 in a horrible car crash on the Ohio Turnpike, Danielle cried uncontrollably for a month. The death of her parents was devastating for her, but what hurt more was that she had never told them the truth about her lifestyle choices and her lifelong emotional troubles. In fact, she had never told her real secrets to anyone at all.

The short shuttle ride to the ship was uneventful. The view of the massive ship was impressive as they neared and boarding her went very quickly.

As Danielle walked to the Windjammer with her friends to have a bite to eat before meeting Jake, she wasn't sure if she could tell them her own secrets.

*****

During their final high school year, the JMH seniors had seen their beloved Cleveland Browns win a championship as Gary Collins, Frank Ryan, and Lou Groza became household names not just in Cleveland but nationally. Their Cleveland Indians were showing some promise too, with Vic Davalillo and Rocky Colavito providing the power and veterans Dick Donovan and Sonny Siebert leading the pitching staff that included promising newcomers like Sam McDowell and Luis Tiant. It was a great time to be a Cleveland sports fan. Even the Cleveland Barons, the hockey team in the American Hockey League, was viewed as the seventh best hockey team in the country.

At John Marshall in their senior year, Jake had pitched his JMH baseball team to a West Senate championship with Bruce as his hard-hitting third baseman. For their final summer before college, Jake already had landed a part-time job at Malley's Ice Cream in nearby Lakewood. Michelle, who didn't especially appreciate that Jake was going to be a soda jerk because of all the girls that were hanging out at Malley's, would spend her summer translating for tourist groups at the ethnic gardens at Rockefeller Park. Bruce was going to be an intern for a local electrical contractor, and Barbara landed an internship at a local veterinarian's office, where her skills with a microscope were more than welcomed.

For Jake, Michelle, Barbara, and Bruce, the senior prom was the coup de grâce of high school. It was even-more important than their commencement ceremony that would take place a week after the prom. It was a given that the four of them were going to win a lot of awards, and some of them would have to deliver commencement speeches, which John Cihlar would have to censor. They all wondered what would become of Danielle. Why wasn't she going to college? Why is she still with Ron? Why is she avoiding all their attempts to remain her friend? Should they remind her that she is a talented artist, or would she view that as patronizing?

As the day approached, Jake and Bruce wondered if prom night would be the night that they would finally lose their virginities. Both had come close, having reached second base and even third base on occasion, but as they rounded third, they were playfully stopped by

Michelle and Barbara, who quickly turned the intimacy into a discussion of the Indians' current slump. Guys using the thought of baseball to extend their staying power was something Jake and Bruce mused as they realized what the girls were doing to them!

Jake and Bruce were already prepared for the big event as proven by their courage when they walked into a drugstore just before closing (so nobody else was there) to purchase rubbers, which they proudly stashed in their wallets just in case! The truth, though, was that the only time the rubbers were ever seen was when Jake and Bruce wanted to prove to their horny friends that they were getting a lot of action. No, their friends never believed them and then tormented them with their cures for blue balls!

Michelle, Danielle, and Barbara once discussed their virginity together after a night that featured the sipping of a few beers that Barbara served the group from her dad's well-stocked refrigerator.

"But what if I get pregnant?" Barbara queried.

"What if the rubber breaks?" asked Michelle as both she and Barb laughed cautiously at that possibility.

Danielle said nothing at all and seemed distracted during the important discussion. As Barbara and Michelle shared their laugh, they wondered together how much longer the guys could hold out without sex but also knew that if they didn't give in, the relationships with their boyfriends would probably not last once they went to college. Is that what the girls wanted?

The JMH senior prom of 1965 was held in the ballroom of the Marriott Hotel in Downtown Cleveland. The after-prom was held at the Trisket Party Center just off W. 140th Street, awfully close to the high school. The prom was from 8:00 p.m. until midnight, with most couples dining beforehand in a fancy downtown Cleveland restaurant. Many ate at the Theatrical Restaurant, a hot spot on Short Vincent Street, often patronized by George Steinbrenner, a rich businessman who many hoped would buy the Cleveland Indians.

Most of the students had saved for months to rent limousines and tuxedos and to buy appropriate corsages and dresses. Tickets for the prom itself were $20 each, and a ticket for the after-prom was $10, but that included a breakfast prepared by the proud parents and teachers of the attendees. As almost always happened, the big issue was whether a JMH senior could invite someone from another high school as a date. Tradition said no. But this year Henry Viper, as class president, said yes, and thus he flaunted his power as the head of the senior class, mainly to his own advantage. His date was a twenty-one-year-old girl, obviously not a JMH student that few had ever seen, named Trudy Gimbol. She was being nonaffectionally called Gimbol the Bimbo by the less-mature JMH senior boys. They spent the night glaring at her extreme cleavage and asking if she could fix them up with someone like her!

The cost of a prom ticket and the large graduation class of over 750 allowed the senior-class officers to bring in a top local band for the prom. A new group was catching on in Cleveland named The Outsiders. The band was led by east-siders, Tom King and Sonny Geraci. The Outsiders gladly played the prom for a price of $250 and as many girls' phone numbers and panties as they could collect. The group got standing ovations as even the clunky guys danced to many of their songs, including two called *Respectable* and *Time Won't Let Me*. The latter went on to become a top 5 song nationally in 1966, and Geraci went on to form the band, Climax, who subsequently released the song *Precious and Few,* another gigantic hit still viewed today as a classic, easy-listening song. Geraci returned to Cleveland in 1980 to star in the Shaker Heights adult softball league, where his teammates included Jake who had always admired Geraci as a man and as a talented singer.

The music of The Outsiders was great, but the slow dances at the prom were hypnotizing for the "almost adults" who were squeezing each other tight and wondering if tonight was going to be *the night* that they officially became men and women. Michelle was stunning on prom night, and Jake was not the only one who noticed her. She was spectacular. Her hair was long and flowing. Her bangs still came to her eyebrows, and her breasts extended like the firmest but softest intrusions into her low-cut dress. Her dress was off-white and didn't quite reach her knees. As Jake peered at this goddess, he knew that she just might be the one for him forever. When the DJ played *My Girl*, the great hit by The Temptations, Michelle melted into Jake's arms. Everybody noticed, especially Henry Viper, who no longer seemed interested in Gimbol the Bimbo. To no one's surprise, Henry was crowned prom king, and Frenchy Valour was crowned the prom queen probably because she was showing a lot more cleavage than the other candidates were willing to show on this magical night. Most high school kids during the sixties knew who the class slut was, and Frenchy was professionally qualified for that honor.

After his coronation, Henry Viper felt invincible. He had become the president of the senior class and the prom king all in the same school year. He felt like royalty. He felt as if he could have anything that he wanted. With a boldness that he always seemed to have, Henry walked up to Michelle and asked her to dance.

"Michelle, I would be honored if the most-beautiful girl at the prom would give me the next dance. After all, Michelle, you would be dancing with both a president and a king," boasted Henry.

"No, thanks," answered Michelle as politely as she could. "If you haven't noticed, I'm taken, and I don't think Jake would approve. Trudy will be back soon, and tradition says you should be dancing with Frenchy. After all, she is the prom queen."

Michelle remained calm and collected but could see the anger simmering in Henry's eyes.

Henry was shocked by the rejection. He wasn't used to the word no. He wasn't used to being turned down by anyone. How could she not want to dance with me? he thought.

"Screw you, bitch, you don't know what you're missing," he yelled as he stomped back to Trudy Gimbol.

As the prom ended, the attendees had two hours before the after prom started. Some were checked into hotels to try to lose their virginity. Others returned to their cars to get a quick drink from the flasks they couldn't smuggle into the dance. Others cried as they suffered the consequences of a horrible evening, and still others wondered why they had even bothered to come to what was supposed to be the best night of their lives. Most chose to return home to check with their parents and to change clothes to ready themselves for the after-prom. Jake and Bruce were on the cleanup committee, so they arranged to pick Michelle and Barb up at Michelle's house around 1:45 a.m. Michelle's parents planned to leave around 1:00 to get to the party center to serve as after-prom chaperones. As Jake, Bruce, Barb, and Michelle, finalized their plans, they did not notice that Henry Viper was listening to every word they said. After changing their clothes, Jake and Bruce would pick up Barb then head to Michelle's as they would drive together to the wonderful after-party.

When Michelle arrived home, she hugged her parents and told them that the night was wonderful beyond comprehension. Her smile brought tears of joy to the hearts of her parents, both of whom were language professors at Case Western Reserve University. It was no secret why Michelle loved foreign languages. Michelle's mom and dad left the house at 1:00 a.m. to assume their jobs as chaperones and kissed their daughter goodbye. The front door remained unlocked, and they did not notice the darkened car parked in front of their house.

Michelle quickly jumped into the shower to scrub the smell of sweat, expensive perfume, and prom wear and tear from her body. She was happy. She was smiling. She sang *Time Won't Let Me* as if she was Sonny Geraci's backup singer. As she thought about the lyrics, which included the words, "I can't wait forever," she decided that somehow, someway, she was going to grant Jake his wish tonight. She was also sure that he had bought some rubbers! As that thought spun in her head, she heard the front door open and heard the steps of someone entering her home.

"Barb, is that you?" There was no answer. "Jake?" Again, there was no answer. She wrapped a towel around herself and walked to the living room. "Mom, did you forget something?"

Michelle was shocked and terrified to see an intruder. He was dressed in all black, had a ski mask covering his head, and was holding a gun. The first words out of his mouth were, "Shut up. If you make a sound, I will kill you, and if you tell a soul about this, I'll murder your family. Just shut your fucking mouth and enjoy the ride. I know I will." He then proceeded to rape her violently. As he left the home, he uttered, "Don't forget, don't tell a soul, or your family's dead!"

It was over in just minutes. It was violent. It was painful. The slaps to Michelle's face drew some blood. She didn't fight back. She placed herself into a self-induced trance to hide the pain that was as much mental as it was physical. As the rapist left, she stared at him, and even though his disguise hid him well, she was sure that she recognized his voice. Could Henry Viper have done this to me? she thought to herself as she shook, cried, and went into a shock that she would never overcome.

*****

As the *Allure* was leaving Fort Lauderdale, headed for Sint Maarten, Bruce, Barbara, Ron, and Danielle joined Jake at the Riding Tides bar and caught up on their lives since they had last seen each other at Michelle's funeral back in 1975. They had avoided high school reunions since Michelle's suicide because they could not stand the reality that she wouldn't be there. They also hated discussing the entire question of what had happened to her and how they had all played a part. Only Jake and Barbara knew the truth. But they had all decided to come together now to discuss avenging her death no matter what. Nothing else mattered.

Chapter 6

After a lot of catching up and reminiscing with his friends, Jake brought up the night of the senior prom. Were their signs at the prom that something was bothering Michelle? Did any of them feel that Michelle was uncomfortable about something at the after-prom? Was someone leering at Michelle? If something was wrong, how could we all have missed it? These were questions Jake posed to his friends, thinking that maybe they had an inkling of what happened to her on that awful night. He wondered if they had possibly seen what he had missed and wasn't aware of until years later.

*****

After Henry Viper left her house, Michelle laid on the floor for five minutes without moving. She was in shock. When tears began to pour from her eyes, she began to realize what had just happened to her. She noticed small amounts of blood dripping from her face. She ran to the bathroom to wash away any sign of blood in hopes that no one would notice. What was she going to say when Jake, Barbara, and Bruce arrived to take her to the after-prom? Her thought was that she would reveal nothing. If they noticed the mark on her face, she would explain that she merely slipped in the shower as the after-effect of too much spiked punch at the prom. While showering again to wash away the scent of her rapist, she noticed the bruises and cuts were over a good part of her body. How was she going to explain any of this? She scrubbed and scrubbed, rubbing her skin raw, but it didn't seem to help.

Just as Michelle was finishing her second shower, Jake, Barbara, and Bruce walked into the house. They were dressed in comfortable clothes perfect for dancing and eating a dressed-down breakfast at the party center.

When he heard the shower running, Jake yelled out, "Hey, Michelle, hurry up, or I may just decide to run in and join you."

Bruce and Barbara laughed, and they both joined in, saying, "You should be so lucky, Jake."

As she pulled herself together, Michelle yelled back, "Be right there." She quickly dressed into some comfortable sweats that effectively covered up most of her bruised body. She applied extra makeup to her face that was already starting to swell, and she tried her best to put on a smiling face as she joined her friends.

Barbara was the first to notice that Michelle had not been successful in covering up her bruises.

"Michelle, are you okay?" she blurted out with a voice filled with concern.

Michelle didn't know what to say as she flinched when Jake kissed her. She knew she had to say something.

"Nothing, guys. I just slipped in the shower. I was in such a rush to get ready that I guess I was just clumsy in there. But I'm fine and ready to continue the best night ever. It's so great to be together with all of you. You are the best friends that a girl could ever have." But nothing could hide her eyes, red from crying.

Jake seemed satisfied with the answer, but he also sensed that she wasn't telling them the whole story. As the group walked to their cars, Jake looked at Bruce and saw a look of concern on his usually joyful face. Barbara just knew that something had happened to Michelle and made it her point to find out.

As the foursome entered the party center, Michelle immediately saw her mom and dad. Realizing that she could not avoid them, she quickly went up to them, using the cover of the very dark room to hide her bruises. She kissed them and verified that her night had been perfect and that all was well in her world. Her parents, partially distracted by the glitz of the evening, didn't notice that Michelle was suffering far more than they would ever know.

The Triskett party center was adorned with decor appropriate for the occasion. Red and white crepe paper filled the room in honor of the school colors of JMH. Trophies won by the senior class were put on display, and the names of the Most Likely list were revealed for the first time. Jake and Michelle won the Cutest Couple award. Barbara won the Most Likely to Succeed category while Bruce won the award for the Guy Most Likely to Become a Member of the Cleveland Indians. Danielle won the category of Most Likely to Have an Exhibit at the Cleveland Museum of Art, along with the award for the Most Likely to Top Andy Warhol for Pop Art Displays that Nobody Could Understand. Danielle was the only award winner not there to accept her trophy along with the ribbing that went with all the honors. Henry was seen escorting Gimbol the Bimbo into the men's room in hopes of having his second conquest of the evening. He was also hoping that this one would be consensual and that he would not have to resort to violence to make it happen.

As the music for the evening was cranking up, the energy of the seniors was apparent. Perhaps they had all stopped after the prom to imbibe in some liquid refreshment, or maybe they were just eighteen-year-olds who were in the best shape of their lives and could easily dance the night away and then sleep for a week. It was their day. It was their time. They wanted to enjoy it. Michelle, though, was the exception, and no one noticed it more than Barbara.

When Jake and Bruce left the table to talk to some of their old buddies, Barbara looked at Michelle and said, "Michelle, we've known each other for a long time. I can tell when something's wrong with you. What happened after the prom to cause your bruises? Please don't lie to me. I know something happened."

Michelle gazed at Barbara with a look of dread on her face, a face that was quickly covered with tears that were dripping down her cheeks.

"Barb, I'm sorry. I already told you. I slipped in the shower."

"I don't believe you," Barbara snapped back at her in a voice filled with concern. "I think someone hurt you. I think somebody hurt you badly. I'm your friend, Michelle. Please let me help you."

Michelle was now sobbing out of control but composed herself enough to grab Barbara's hand and say, "Let's step outside and talk, but you have to promise to never tell anyone else what I am going to tell you." Barbara agreed.

As the two good friends walked out into the cool May evening, often the norm for Cleveland, Ohio, Michelle wondered if she could tell Barb the truth. She looked around to see if Henry Viper noticed her, worrying that he would know that she was divulging the awful truth to Barbara. Truth can be painful, and Barb wondered if she would have the ability to support her best friend. Both realized that they were becoming adults, and that was supposed to come with an inner strength and wisdom that younger high school age kids didn't have. Both Michelle and Barb were hoping that they could act like adults.

"I was raped, Barb, at my house right after I got out of the shower before you guys picked me up," said Michelle whose tears were flowing again.

She felt a sense of relief when she said those words out loud for the first time. Some of her pain went away as she said them. The pain was being replaced by rage!

"Oh my god, Michelle. I am so sorry," Barb uttered, knowing that she had no idea what to think or what to say next. The two young women hugged each other tightly and, after parting, looked at each other with the love and concern of true friends. "Michelle, you know that I have a lot of questions, but I will never force you to talk about any of this if you don't want to. I will always be there to support you and help you with anything you need. Please just ask me. You shouldn't go through this alone. I want to help," Barb said.

"Thanks, Barb. Right now I have no idea what I'm going to do. I think I know who did it, but I'm not quite sure. He was disguised, but I'm sure I recognized his voice. I don't want my parents to know because they'll launch an investigation or call the police. I don't want any of that. I just want things to return to normal. I want my last summer before college to be fun and filled with the joys of life, and that includes hanging around with Jake and you and Bruce and Danielle before we leave for college. But what is most frightening, Barb, is that he also said that if I ever said anything to anyone, he would kill my family."

As Michelle said those words, she burst into tears again. Barb whispered that she understood and hugged Michelle tightly again before they reentered the Triskett Center. As she dried her eyes, Michelle looked around to see if Henry Viper had seen her talking to Barb.

Jake and Bruce had been spending a big part of the evening talking to many of their oldest friends who were all seated together, mostly dateless, at a table that seemed reserved for the kids that didn't fit into any category. In 1965 high school groups consisted of the brainiacs, the jocks, and the others. The others included kids who were physically immature, kids who barely made it through high school, kids who had to work after school because their parents couldn't support their family, kids who smoked and drank a lot, kids preparing to enter the military service to prepare for Vietnam, and kids who preferred listening to country music instead of The Beatles. Jake and Bruce knew a lot of these guys; and on one hand, they were happy that they weren't still part of any of these groups, but on the other hand, they liked these guys a lot and wanted to spend time with them as their high school days were ending.

So the fun began as Jake and Bruce and the gang traded stories that were often funny and usually gross. Jake reminded Jim Manley how he was awestruck when he saw Jim's pubic hair for the first time when the boys disrobed after gym class during sixth grade. Jim was always very mature for his age.

Mark Roundhouse told the story about going to the Cleveland Arena to see a championship wrestling match featuring Dick the Bruiser and The Sheik.

"Yeah, back then I really thought professional wrestling was real," pleaded Mark, "until I saw our wrestling coach, Fred Gibbons, playing poker with both the Bruiser and The Sheik in the back room of the arena after most of the crowd had left."

Gibbons was the legendary wrestling coach at JMH who moonlighted as the main referee for the pro wrestlers as well as one of their main scriptwriters.

Jack Hickman, who stilled lived across the street from Jake, discussed the merits of country music and why he chose to play the slide guitar instead of the accordion.

"Because it gets me those wild country girls," said Jack as his friends pointed out that he was dateless for the prom.

And Eddie Baptist, who was off to culinary school in Connecticut, was wondering if he could keep his girlfriend, Tammy, when he left town to become a chef.

"I think I love her," said Eddie, "but my parents are telling me that I'm too young to get married right now. They want me to get through culinary school first and then get married. Well, damn it, I love Tammy, and I want to marry her and take her to Connecticut with me."

Just as Eddie said that, Tammy returned to the table, admitted that she heard what he said, and exclaimed, "Let's elope, Eddie!" The table went wild.

Bruce was the first to see that Michelle and Barb were reentering the party center.

"Hey, Jake, it's time to get back to our women," he said with a note of reluctance since he was enjoying the laughter with his old friends.

"Okay, let's do it," replied Jake. "Let's show them that their four years trying to teach us how to dance weren't wasted."

As the couples reunited, Jake could sense that something was wrong. Bruce noticed this as well, but neither of them could put their finger on it. Did they do something wrong? Did the girls not enjoy the evening? Or were they all only tired, and it was hitting them that their youth was quickly ending?

*****

They would have two nights at sea before the *Allure of the Seas* reached Sint Maarten. Danielle, Barbara, Jake, Bruce, and Ron spent most of that time together. Seeking a quiet place to discuss Jake's plan, they decided to eat their dinner at Chops, one of the specialty restaurants on the ship. Barbara had booked a luxurious suite as her cabin, so they utilized it for much of their discussion. As they talked about the night of the prom, Barbara and Jake felt it was time to tell their friends the truth and explain why they were really on this ship at this exact time. Ron was happy that the truth was finally coming out. Barb spoke first.

"On the night of our prom," Barb blurted out quickly, "Michelle was raped at her house as she was changing out of her dress. She told me at the after-prom."

"And we know who did it!" exclaimed Jake. "He's on this ship, and we're going to kill him! Barb and I hope that all of you will agree to help us."

Chapter 7

Bruce and Danielle were startled by the news of Michelle's rape on the night of their senior prom.

"Is this why you asked us to join you?" asked Bruce.

Danielle shifted in her seat and said, "Do you really expect us to help you?" She had a bit of disgust in her voice, which could be expected from a flower child, even one who was almost seventy years old.

"*Yes!* We certainly hope you will," Jake rapidly exclaimed. "We owe it to Michelle to avenge her death. After she was raped, her life fell apart, and she was never the same. We all saw that. I loved her. I had hopes of marrying her and raising kids with her, but she never gave me the chance to get close to her after that night. I never knew why. I figured I must have done something wrong even though I simply couldn't think of anything I did. I never knew what the problem was between us. She withdrew, and when she totally rejected me, I gave up on her. I never saw Michelle again after the summer of '65 when I made the effort to visit her in Pittsburgh until I saw her in her casket."

"Barb, why didn't you tell us?" said Bruce as Danielle looked as if she was going to either be sick or burst into tears or maybe both.

"I couldn't tell anyone. Michelle made me promise that I would never tell a soul. She said she was okay and that she could handle it on her own and move on. But what she really feared was that the rapist would kill her family if she ever told anyone. I'm sure the pressure of keeping this quiet created the stress that led to her suicide. We were her best friends. We had great lives. It's time that we do the right thing and make this right."

Barb's passion reminded all of them how remarkable she really was. Barb had been their valedictorian. She had graduated with honors from Ohio State and had practiced medicine in Cleveland and in Houston for almost forty years. Her work on AIDS prevention won worldwide attention, and some even talked about her winning the Nobel Prize in Medicine.

So, after Barb's impassioned plea, Bruce and Danielle looked at each other and sensed that they, too, had a new mission in life. They would join Jake and Barbara to avenge Michelle's death. Sometimes being a vigilante might be justified, and this was one of those times.

And then Bruce looked at Ron and asked, "And what about you, Ron? Will you help too?"

Startling the old friends, Ron exclaimed, "You better believe it, Bruce. Nothing is more important to me right now than helping all of you. No, we can't bring her back, but we can even the score. She deserves that."

*****

The JMH class of 1965 officially graduated on June 5, 1965, after a hot, humid day that included intermittent showers. The ceremony was held in the football stadium where past glories were remembered and future ones were certain to occur. Principal Cihlar raved about the accomplishments of the class, bragging that 67 percent of their 785 grads were already accepted into colleges. As the class president, Henry Viper spoke about the value of his time in student government and suggested that he might take his skills to another level. Barb, the valedictorian and Bruce's longtime love, spoke about the challenges ahead for the class of '65 and ended her speech by shouting the class slogan, "Forever onward." Jake was voted to be the senior-class speaker, something he always believed was one of the greatest honors of his life, and that fact made him apply to be a senior advisor when he later taught at JMH. He loved the pomp and circumstance of the ceremony and wanted it to live on forever. Jake talked about the friendships that had been made, the love that the seniors had for each other, and the appreciation they all had for the hardworking teachers who watched them grow up into almost-adults. Jake wished all of them well.

Near the end of his speech, Jake was interrupted as track star, Jimmy Kish, slipped out of his cap and gown and streaked naked past the entire entourage of parents, special guests, and grandparents. Even Principal Cihlar got a laugh at that senior prank. After the crowd settled down and Jimmy was taken away by security, 785 names were called as each accepted their diploma. Parents cheered, students cried, many photos were taken, and mortar boards were tossed into the air. When the JMH choir sang *The Lord Bless You and Keep You*, the class of 1965 was officially dismissed to enter the world.

Many of the parents of the class of '65 hosted graduation parties for their aspiring movers and shakers. Bragging rights were often in order as the parents proudly discussed the accomplishments of their children while not listening to the other adults who were bragging about their own kids. Danielle's parents insisted on hosting a party not only because their wealth made it mandatory in their circles but also to shame their daughter into going to college.

"Mom, thank you for doing this, but I am not going to change my mind," said Danielle as the topic came up day after day.

While her parents planned the party, Danielle's mom just kept on trying. Her plan was to wear down her daughter, and maybe then Danielle would agree to further her education just to shut her mom up. "Okay, mom, I'll think about it, but only if you let me spike the punch for the party," she countered with a bit of a smile even though she had no intention of ever changing her mind. She figured her friends did expect a little alcohol at the party. She knew her mom was easy and would always give her anything she wanted.

Danielle's graduation party was the highlight of the summer of '65 for the graduates of JMH. Games were played, and stories were told that were filled with exaggerations and outright lies. Food and drink were consumed in large quantities. Loud music interrupted the sleep of the animals in the close by metro parks, and longtime romances were fortified that night as well as destroyed. Danielle had not spoken to Ron in person since he slapped her after their fight about going to the prom. Encouraged by Michelle, Jake, Bruce, and

Barb, she called up the courage to attend the after-prom and wondered what she would say to Ron if he showed up. He didn't.

Three hours into Danielle's party, Ron Bloodstone knocked on Danielle's door and was welcomed in by Henry Viper who had been there since the beginning and was already very drunk.

"How's that fucking mom of yours, Ron? Uncle Johnny told me yesterday that she's still the best lay he's ever had. You ought to be so proud, Ron. I mean, wow, you get to see her every day. You're so damn lucky."

Ron glared at Henry but pulled back as he thought about what would happen if he hit him. Ron was very composed as he calmly told Henry that all was forgiven. He knew that his mother was a terrible human being, and she was the reason that his father was in jail.

Speaking slowly and calmly, Ron said, "Look, Henry, I get it. If she wants to fuck you and fuck your uncle Johnny, that is her fucking business, not mine. I get it, I get it, I get it! Henry, she's a whore. My father knew it, and I've known it for most of my life. That's not your fault. Just keep me out of it."

Henry was both sobered and shocked by what he was hearing and didn't know how to answer.

"But Henry," Ron continued, "I'm here to talk to Danielle. I'm leaving home and enlisting in the army. I need to tell her. Do you know where she is?"

Henry, looking really confused, wordlessly pointed Ron in the direction of the backyard where Danielle was being a gracious hostess.

Ron found her sitting at a picnic table with Barb. They were seemingly involved in a serious, quiet conversation. He also saw Bruce and Jake in another part of the yard and immediately wondered why Michelle was nowhere to be seen. As Ron approached the girls, he said, "Excuse me, Barb, could I have a private word with Danielle?"

Barb looked at Danielle for her approval and received a quick nod before she felt she could leave them alone.

But as she turned, she said, "Talk it out, guys. Danielle, you just yell if you need me."

Ron spoke first, "Danielle, ever since I slapped you, I haven't slept. I'm miserable. I want you to know that's not me. I'm not that kind of a guy. I play the part of a tough guy, but you must know that's not really me at all. You've made me understand how stupid I am. I tried to change for you. I put in a good effort, but sometimes I just lose it. I can't explain why. I don't understand it myself. Yes, I am sorry and hope that you'll forgive me. I know that I need to grow up. I know that you think I'm crazy and immature. Yes, I am. I know that, so I'm here not only to apologize but to give you some news to show you how serious I am about changing my life."

Danielle listened closely to every word, as if she knew that once she heard what Ron had to say, she might have to make a decision that could change her life. Was she ready for all the possibilities?

"Danielle," Ron continued, "I've enlisted in the army. I leave for boot camp in two weeks, and then, most likely, I'll be sent to Vietnam."

Ron was nervously shaking when he said those words. He hadn't told anyone yet. His mother could care less what he did, and he only got to visit his dad once a month.

She immediately began to stare into Ron's beautiful blue eyes and realized that he probably was a good guy who had been dealt an awfully bad hand in life. Danielle grabbed him and hugged him as tightly as she had ever embraced anyone in her life.

"Of course, I forgive you, Ron. You've meant so much to me since we met, and I understand why you are the way you are. But I have to tell you something too."

"What is it?" wondered Ron.

"I really didn't mind when you teased me about my art. I know it's strange. Sometimes I don't even understand it myself. And I totally understand why you get frustrated when I reject your advances. I get the wants and needs of guys our age." Danielle paused and took a deep breath as if she had to compose herself before she continued. "Ron, I think I like girls. I think I may be a lesbian!".

He immediately pulled back from Danielle's embrace and stared at her in disbelief.

"What? How do you know? Have you done it with a girl? Are you sure? How can you be a dyke? How can you be a Gillette blade?" he said, slightly raising his voice.

Ron's confusion started to amuse Danielle.

"Ron, keep your voice down. No, I am not sleeping with a woman and never have, and no, I'm not sure if I ever will. You're the first person I've ever told."

Ron was slowly absorbing Danielle's words and started to laugh out loud. This was hardly the reaction that she had expected.

"So, it wasn't me!" Ron said with a tinge of pride.

"No, Ron. Rock Hudson could have come to my house with the intention of seducing me, and I would have rejected him."

Both laughed out loud. They'd now shared secrets with each other that were so personal their bond, stronger than ever, was exploding inside each of them.

As they walked together to join the others, he asked Danielle if she had heard anything about Michelle.

"Why wasn't she here at your party?" he wondered out loud.

Danielle knew extraordinarily little, only that rumors were circulating that Jake and Michelle were having a tough time. Michelle wasn't answering phone calls, and some of their friends thought that she might be leaving for Pittsburgh early to start classes at Carnegie Mellon during the summer session.

Ron and Danielle noticed that Jake, Bruce, and Barb were talking together in a corner of the large yard.

"Why don't we ask them?" suggested Danielle.

"Hey, Jake, that was quite a stunt, having Jimmy Kish streak just as you were finishing your speech," said Ron.

"Thanks," Jake laughed, "but it would have been much more fun if Gloria Morningstar did it instead. With her large boobs, she would have bounced. Jimmy only flopped."

They all laughed out loud. Feeling like he was finally fitting in with all them, Ron asked about Michelle. He seemed sincerely concerned and wondered why she wasn't at the party. Barb's face immediately showed a combination of fear and uncertainly. She said nothing. Bruce merely shrugged his shoulders.

Jake simply answered by saying, "I wish we knew."

*****

As the discussion aboard the *Allure* continued, a consensus was mustered as to how Bruce and Danielle would help. Ron's role in the plan was yet to be laid out. Jake and Barb had planned the gig for the last two years ever since Jake considered the possibility of retribution at their fiftieth high school reunion. Barb had told Jake about the rape five years after Michelle's funeral. The news was hard to divulge for Barb since she had promised never to tell anyone, but she felt that Jake deserved to know since Michelle was gone. What harm would it be for him to know? When Jake got the news of the rape of his high school sweetheart, a rage filled his heart, and he knew that someday he would get revenge. Michelle deserved that and so much more.

Chapter 8

Bruce, Danielle, and Ron were shocked, perplexed, and annoyed all at the same time as Barb and Jake shared Michelle's horrible tale.

"Why didn't you tell us sooner?" asked Bruce.

"You know that we would have helped you. Michelle wasn't only your friend. We loved her too," stated Danielle, who was silently contemplating if she could really endorse a violent act, let alone actually participate in one. "Barb, did Michelle ever confide in you about who the rapist was?"

"No. I tried everything that I could think of to make her tell me, but she said that she was too afraid to do so. I even worked hard to convince her to go to the police, but again, she feared not only for her life but for the life of her family. It wasn't until Jake found out who raped her that we decided to do something about it, and we immediately thought that you guys would help. You don't know how miserable Michelle was after the rape. When she stopped talking to us after the prom, we all should have been more sensitive to what was going on with her, but we weren't. We were casting her out of our own worlds without realizing it. That's on us, and we need to remedy that," argued Barb, as if she was doubting her own words because seeking revenge might also end her life as she knew it along with the lives of her four coconspirators.

"Jake, how did you find out who the rapist was?" queried Bruce.

"I found out at our fiftieth reunion from a very unlikely source."

"Well, who was it, Jake? You've got to tell us," Danielle said with a voice too loud not to be heard by others.

"I told him!" uttered Ron. "It was Henry Viper. He bragged about it to me." Bruce and Danielle were stunned but not really surprised to have their long-held beliefs—that Henry was a lowlife—confirmed.

"I immediately called Barb," said Jake, "and for the last two years, we've been working together to find a way to fix this wrong. Henry is on this ship right now! He doesn't know we're here too, so be sure to avoid him."

Both Danielle and Bruce were stunned at the news. As the thought of evening the score for Michelle sunk in, they at first were disappointed that their friends had not confided in them sooner but quickly agreed that whatever Jake and Barb wanted them to do was both necessary and acceptable.

*****

The summer of 1965 was an exceptionally long one for Jake. Michelle did go off to Pittsburgh early without a good explanation of why she was leaving before she really had to. Her behavior was different. Her spunk had left her, and her desire to talk to him about anything had vanished. Jake wondered if she was taking drugs. He wondered if she was having second thoughts about going to school at all. He wondered if he had done something to offend her. Her inhibitions increased about many things. Her sense of adventure had left her. She was no longer fun. She no longer laughed. And Jake no longer slept, worrying about her.

One weekend in early July Jake drove to Carnegie Mellon to visit Michelle. She had agreed to the visit with a lot of reluctance. That really bothered him.

Filled with trepidation, when he arrived at Michelle's spartan-like dormitory room, Jake didn't know what to expect. Michelle greeted him coldly. There was no hug, no kiss, and a very insincere,

"How are you?" She asked Jake to sit down on her bed, but Jake knew that this would not lead to any physical activity other than a hoped-for heartfelt conversation, which was all that he was really hoping for.

Jake didn't know what to say even though he had contemplated this meeting for weeks.

Finally, he uttered, "Michelle, have I lost you? Are we done? Did I do something wrong? Is it over with for us?"

She immediately burst into tears that evolved into sobs.

"Jake, I love you. I can't explain any of this even to myself. It makes no sense. But I have changed, and right now it would be better for both of us if we just stopped seeing each other."

Jake was stunned.

"What?" Jake quietly whispered. "Am I hearing this correctly? What happened? What did I do? Yes, I love you too. Are you sure about this? Is there someone else? If there is, just tell me."

"No, Jake, there's nobody else. In fact, I think about you constantly, and I'm wondering if this is the right decision for me to make. I just need time. I need to be alone. Being away from you is going to be difficult. I know that. So maybe all I'm saying to you is that since I can't give you all of me right now, I don't want to see you at all."

Michelle said these words, knowing that every word she was saying was a blatant lie.

"Maybe our time apart will change all that. Maybe I'll regret my decision, but Jake, growing up is hard. When you're alone with yourself and deciding what to do with your life, you need to listen to your inner voice. It's no longer times for fun and games and living in a pretend world without consequences. Jake, I need to be in a world without you for a while before I'm certain that I want you to be the biggest part of my life."

Michelle was baring her soul right in front of him.

Jake wanted to cry. He wanted to run away. He wanted to shout as loudly as he could that Michelle was wrong. He felt like he had taken a right cross on the chin from Cassius Clay or Sonny Liston.

"So if I asked you right now to marry me, what would your answer be?" asked Jake.

Michelle did not hesitate with her answer, "It would be no." She responded as if she knew the question was coming. "Jake, we need to see if we're really meant for each other, and the only way to do that is to be apart and see if absence really does make the heart grow fonder."

Jake expected her response and started to believe that everything she said to him that day was part of some scripted act that she had rehearsed but did not want to be a part of. He knew that she was lying about everything she said. He just didn't know why. That was the last time Jake saw Michelle alive.

Barb and Bruce spent the summer working, going to amusement parks, including Euclid Beach, Cedar Pont, and to Geauga Lake. They especially loved to ride the roller coasters. They were thrilled at the announcement that Sea World was going to open a second park in the Cleveland area at about the time of their college graduations. Barb said that it might be fun to become a veterinarian instead of a people doctor because animals don't complain as much nor sue as much as people do. Bruce kidded that maybe he could run her hospital. They went to concerts at Leo's Casino and marveled at the stylings of the Four Tops, The Temptations, and The Supremes and at the wit of Richard Pryor and Flip Wilson. Leo's sat about seven hundred patrons and was one of the places in Cleveland where your race, creed, or color didn't matter. The times they were a-changing—something promised to all by Bob Dylan, the voice of the younger generation.

After Labor Day, when the departure time for college was near, Jake, Bruce, and Barb had one final day to say goodbye. They drove out to Edgewater Park, swam in the seventy-two-degree water of Lake Erie, knowing that it was very polluted from industrial waste. They had a picnic lunch, drank a little beer, and lamented that Michelle, Ron, and Danielle were not with them. Danielle had thought about joining them but was going to attend Ron's celebration for getting through boot camp. He was processed in Ann Arbor, Michigan, and was being sent off to Fort Knox in Kentucky. He had quit smoking and drinking after high school and was proud to finish boot camp near the top of his class in the armor division. He even regretted how much of his life he had screwed up by being a jerk in high school and by being led into a life of crime by Henry Viper. Danielle was immensely proud of him but didn't have any romantic feelings for him at all. She just wanted to congratulate him for his success. After all, there was no one else who cared, including his family.

Sometimes the friends you make in high school will become your lifelong friends. When in school, kids think that their friendships will last forever. Life often takes you on twists and turns that you never saw coming, and you tend to drift apart. But when Jake, Bruce, and Barb were saying goodbye, they hoped that they would see each other often. They had shared much of their youth as best friends. They had experienced things together that they would never forget. As they toasted Ron's success at boot camp, they wondered aloud if they would ever see Michelle again and wondered if Danielle and Ron would end up together. They hoped so because they all thought that they were good for each other.

During his four years at Indiana University, Jake almost totally forgot about Michelle. Maybe she was right after all, he often thought as he was eyeing the latest coed walking down the quad. He wrote to Michelle three times during his freshman year. She never responded. He even called her once after the Hoosier football team won a game over big rival, Purdue, to guarantee a trip to the Rose Bowl. His roommates were in a fun, celebratory mood and dared him to call the girl who none of them had ever met. Obediently, Jake called but became embarrassed and sullen when she didn't answer the phone.

When he came home for Thanksgiving vacation, Jake drove past Michelle's home but didn't knock on her door. When he went to a JMH basketball game the day after Thanksgiving, he saw many of his old classmates, but Michelle was not among them. He did see Barb and Bruce, but only for a few minutes. They, too, were doing well at Ohio State and at Purdue and seemed excited about their lives, but not too excited about seeing Jake. Maybe separation changed people more than Jake ever knew.

When Jake returned to IU, he not only lost touch with Michelle but also with Barb and Bruce. He finally lost his virginity after a party off campus. She was a wild child from Youngstown, Ohio, named Gloria Schwartz. Gloria was Jewish, so when Jake met her, he immediately asked her if she knew Sam and Norm Feinstein from Cleveland. She was perplexed.

"Why would I know them?" she said quietly as if Jake thought that all Jews knew each other.

True, Jake only knew two Jews, the Feinsteins, and only knew them because they were on one of his baseball teams; but after a couple of drinks, he laughed as he realized how stupid he had been for asking such a dumb question.

"Your beauty intimidates me, Gloria. I was just trying to make conversation," he said while displaying a sheepish grin.

She laughed too as she said, "You know what? You are pretty cute for a pollack."

Now they both laughed out loud and gave each other a big hug from one Buckeye to another who were sitting in Hoosier land.

As Jake and Gloria walked back to Reed Quad, Gloria's dorm, they were fully intoxicated. They swerved, fell, staggered, took wrong turns, slurred their words, and were trying their best to get Gloria home before curfew. And then, as they walked through Dunn Meadow and were approaching the Jordan River, which was really a four-foot-wide creek, they seduced each other. The hit song of the day was Van Morrison's *Brown Eyed Girl* whose lyrics included "making love in the green grass with you." Those words embellished Jake's head as a distraction to help him last just a little bit longer before his explosion. It was the first time for both and the last time that they were together. She was only five minutes past curfew!

With his virginity officially vanquished, Jake's days thinking about Michelle did not totally disappear. That really surprised him. He wondered sometimes if he only liked her because of a sexual attraction. He wondered if he fell for Michelle because she had approached him first back at the dance at Baker Middle School many years ago. He was now painfully aware that there were plenty of other fish in the sea, and perhaps experiencing life by becoming friendly with some of the coeds would be the way to go. Yes, he was sexually attracted to many of them, but he knew sex was far from the only thing in a relationship. He did admit to himself that he loved

Michelle for many reasons even though he kept hoping for the sex to blossom. He did muster the courage to call her in Pittsburgh to invite her to see him ride in the Little 500, a bicycle race that is a part of a festive weekend held every spring at IU. She said no. His friends, including roommates Sherman Washington and Gary Dorsey, consoled him on the rejection but continued to rib him about Michelle, the mystery girl that they had never seen. They told him to forget about her as it was obvious that she no longer cared about him.

"She dumped you, Jake. Get over it. Hell, it happens to the best of us. Go ask that lovely Rita to the Little 500," urged Gary.

Jake thought about it but decided to give Michelle one more chance when he returned to Cleveland for the summer.

*****

As the *Allure* docked in Sint Maarten, the newly formed partners in crime decided to go ashore and discuss the plan at the famous Sunset Bar and Grill near the airport where the planes literally fly right over your head. The friends had all gathered on the top deck to watch the ship dock. From their vantage point, they could see welcome bands, fishing boats, men dressed like James Bond, women dressed like starlets, one's own personal paparazzi taking your picture, tour operators who were hucksters, straw markets, street merchants who would sell you anything, and a lot of old buses with oil leaks. All this was part of the atmosphere that most cruisers enjoyed at every port. The group returned to their rooms to prepare for their trip into town.

Ron's presence meant a lot to Danielle and Bruce who were more intrigued then ever as some of this plot began to make sense. They needed to do this not only for Michelle but because they had to repair their friendships, which had been sidetracked by time and distance.

Chapter 9

Sint Maarten was one of the most beautiful places that Jake had ever seen. The view from his balcony as the *Allure* docked was even better than the pictures in travel brochures that were used to entice folks into travelling to the Caribbean. Vintage stores decked out in pastel colors, and royal palms that touched the sky fronted the friendly merchants who were everywhere, wanting to share their lives and their wares with the tourists. This really was a paradise.

As the friends left the ship, checking carefully for Henry's presence, Jake suggested, "Let's make a pact to come back here again when we can really enjoy all this."

The group nodded in agreement. Danielle added that she was inspired to paint the scenery because it was so overwhelming, and Barb wondered if they needed another doctor on the island. Bruce and Ron just gawked at the beautiful women that were everywhere. They took a quick cab ride to the Sunset Bar and Grill, got a table overlooking the sea, and ordered mojitos, their drink of choice while in the Caribbean. After fifteen minutes of small talk, Jake noticed that Ron was staring at Danielle who still looked like she was thirty-something. It was obvious that Ron had never gotten over her. Danielle had not attended the class's fiftieth reunion. Bruce had been there with his wife, Marcia, and Barb, Jake, and Ron were there alone, but Ron purposely avoided people as he hid himself among the many attendees. He only wanted to talk to Jake and finally tell him the identity of Michelle's rapist. Now in Sint Maarten, Ron wasn't sure that he wanted to talk to the entire group because he knew how much they had loved Michelle, and he felt partially responsible for their pain. But it was finally time to get this off his chest.

"Hey, guys. This is as strange for me as it probably is for you. I know that a long time ago, I hurt some of you or maybe even all of you," Ron said as he looked straight at Danielle. "I'm sorry for that. I was an idiotic asshole. In fact, I probably still am. But I want all of you to know that I was wrong and how sorry I am that I may have hurt any of you. I'm here to make things right, and to me, that means eliminating Henry Viper. I've known since Michelle's funeral that Henry raped her. I didn't tell anyone until I told Jake at our fiftieth reunion. Keeping that secret was the worst mistake that I've ever made in my life. I thought that since Michelle was gone, telling you would make no difference to any of you because it wouldn't bring her back. I was wrong. We need to make this right. Michelle deserves that and so much more."

Ron had never spoken with more passion in his entire life. All at the table grimly nodded.

*****

Ron Bloodstone spent two years in Vietnam primarily in the infantry division. He had done most of his training in the armor division, but the jungles of Vietnam made using tanks highly impractical. So Ron was retrained and became a member of the 11th Infantry Brigade. He killed his first man at the Battle of Hill 488; although he wasn't initially aware that he had hit anyone when he had fired his M14 automatic rifle. His unit was heavily involved at Operation Harrison, Operation Paul Revere, and Operation Nathan Hale. During those operations, Ron killed more Vietcong than he could ever count.

"Bloodbaths are a part of the deal," he was told by his lieutenants.

"Your job will get easier after a while," he was told by his captains.

He never believed any of those words. He was haunted by the faces of the Vietcong that he killed, many of whom were only fourteen or fifteen years of age. Even smoking a lot of pot didn't relieve the pain or reduce the guilt and nightmares.

Ron, much like the average infantryman in Vietnam, spent 240 days a year in combat situations. It wasn't like he was shot at daily, but he easily could have been. American helicopters were amazingly effective in moving the troops wherever they were needed. They got the troops in quickly and got them out even faster, especially if there were injured or deceased soldiers. Perhaps the chopper was only moving men to an area that needed to be patrolled, but for a soldier, the uncertainly of every situation was beyond stressful. When combined with an enemy that fought a guerrilla-style war, allies that looked like the enemy and a United States government that seemed uncertain about what course to take, Ron and his fighting brothers were in a war they knew they would probably never win and which seemed idiotic to many of them. 58,148 Americans died in Vietnam, and another 304,000 US soldiers were wounded out of the 2.7 million who served. They all knew that the odds were one in seven that they might die or get injured in Vietnam. He often felt guilty that he had not been one of its victims.

While he was fighting the enemy, Ron got a telegram, telling him that his mother had died of a drug overdose. His thoughts swirled to his time in high school when she was openly screwing every man in town. She'd never been a mother to him, and he had no desire to go back for her funeral. Since his lowlife father was in jail for life and was of no use, all decisions were up to him. He made a quick call back home to have her remains cremated and disposed of and told them that there would be no service and no burial. Upon hearing of the death, his sergeant told Ron to go home, that he was entitled to bereavement time. He just shook his head and went back on duty. He took out his pent-up anger by killing some more Vietcong.

Ron saw plenty of his friends perish. Later in life he attended the funerals of friends who died from the aftereffects of napalm and Agent Orange. As he aged, he resented more and more the fact that he had served in this debacle of a war and that nobody back home seemed to care that he had served his country with honor.

They didn't call it post traumatic syndrome or disorder until 1980, but Ron knew there was something terribly wrong with him when he returned home from the war. Two years in the jungle was enough for him. He chose not to reenlist and hoped that his service in the military would qualify him for a good job back in Cleveland.

He was so very wrong. Being able to drive a tank and shoot a rifle doesn't qualify you for much of any job, he rudely found out. And being the class jerk in school didn't qualify you for anything either. Ron worked at restaurants as a dishwasher. He tried piece work at a local parts factory, and he roamed the country, working small-time carnivals as a ride assembler since he did have some mechanical ability. Nothing pleased him, nothing challenged him, and none of his jobs paid him very well. He was adrift in a turbulent sea. All he could afford was a few dollars to pay the rent on a dilapidated apartment in the Tremont area of Cleveland that was barely dodging the wrecking ball. Combined with his nightmares, his lack of friends, his almost weekly bar fights, and his self-hatred, Ron's miseries grew. When he visited the Veterans hospital in Cleveland, he was told that he would have to wait six months to see a doctor who might help him. He said, "No, thank you!"

In the middle of all his misery, Ron bumped into Henry Viper at a watering hole near the new Marriott Hotel that was going up on W. 150th Street near their old high school. The Red Carpet had been a favorite haunt of Henry since he was eighteen years old even though twenty-one was the legal drinking age. Henry and Ron were now twenty-two, and even the bartender laughed as they discussed how long he had been serving the two friends.

"Oh my god, Henry, what the hell, you're looking good," Ron said as the jukebox belted out *Hot Fun in the Summertime* by Sly & The Family Stone. "Give me a Bud," he said to the bartender, "and give Henry here whatever he wants."

Henry and Ron hugged each other as if they were blood brothers, and then Henry brought up the old times that they had together, and the stories began flowing of the crimes, the treachery, and the bawdy behavior that the two had shared. Ron laughed for the first time since he came home from Nam. It felt good to talk to a friend again. He even had the guts to say to Henry, "And who are you screwing nowadays? I bet she isn't as good as my mom was." They both roared over that one. Little did Henry know that Ron's mom had died an unfortunate death.

As their reunion continued, Ron admitted that he needed a job, that his life was going nowhere, and he wondered if Henry could help him.

"Of course, old buddy," Henry said as he slapped Ron on the back. "I still help Uncle Johnny over in Little Italy, and I know that he's always looking for a good guy to drive his limo and help run the numbers around the east side. He pays well. Would you be interested?"

"God, yes," exclaimed Ron.

"Okay, meet Johnny and me at Therese's Restaurant on Murray Hill about seven tomorrow night, and we'll talk business. And dress well. Johnny likes that a lot," encouraged Henry as he slapped his pal on the back again.

"Thanks so much, Henry," said Ron. "I'll never forget this."

Henry nodded, saying, "And on another note, Ron, did you hear that Jake Markowski just came back to town and is teaching over at Marshall? We ought to go over there and give him some shit and bust his chops just like we used to."

They both roared uncontrollably.

The next day Ron searched his apartment for any loose change to add to the seventeen dollars he had in his wallet. He had to buy a suit to impress Johnny Viper. He ventured to the local Uncle Bill's Department Store and luckily found a suit on sale for fifteen dollars. No, it was not the best-quality suit out there, but Ron looked darn good in it. He'd stayed in shape in the army because he really had no choice, and now it was hard to eat too much back home when you had no money. He was feeling better about himself today than at any time since he'd returned home. With what he hoped was a new zest for life, he decided to visit Danielle.

As Ron pulled into Danielle's parents' home on Rocky River Drive, he wasn't sure if she even lived there anymore; but if she didn't, he knew that her parents would catch him up. He wondered if she was still painting, if she found a girlfriend, or if she'd decided that she wasn't a lesbian after all. Who knows, he might still have a chance. As he rang the doorbell as he smoothed the wrinkles in his new used suit, Ron heard Danielle prancing up to the door. She swung open the heavy door, looked at him, smiled, and gave him a big hug.

"Welcome home, soldier," she blurted out loud, saying the words that Ron hardly ever heard. "You're looking so handsome. Wow, that's a nice suit."

They hugged for a long time, and as they gazed at each other, Ron began to think that his life was turning around. Even if Danielle couldn't be his girlfriend, she at least could be a great friend. That's just what he needed.

The two old friends talked for several hours and would have talked longer, but Ron had that appointment at Theresa's. He apologized for not writing her when he was in Nam, and she apologized for not writing him. She told him she'd asked around to keep up with his whereabouts. Ron told her about the horrors of Nam and the horrors of returning home. He told her about the drugs, about living on the street, how he questioned the government and their reasons for the war, and then he wondered aloud why he could not sleep at night. She listened with a sense of not only interest but also with the compassion that Ron desperately needed.

"Yes, I am a lesbian," Danielle confided in Ron, "but no, there's no one that I'm currently dating. I still paint, and I think I'm getting better. I've even sold some of my work. My parents are immensely proud of what I'm doing and have turned our basement into my studio. They know that I am a lesbian, but they never talk about it with me or especially with our relatives. I guess, for me, it is called living in the closet."

Ron smiled as he compassionately listened to Danielle. When he left, he felt better than he had in years. But a big part of what he was thinking about most was what might have been had things with her been different.

He finally had to excuse himself from their wonderful reunion, stating that he had an appointment for a possible new job. They agreed to keep in touch. Ron reluctantly closed the door behind him and walked to his old jalopy.

Theresa's on Mayfield Road was considered one of the best Italian restaurants in all of Cleveland. It was frequented by gangsters, Cleveland celebrities, and the mafia dons who would ultimately be buried in the Holy Rosary Parish cemetery right down the street. As Ron entered, the wonderful smell of red sauce, pasta, and fresh-baked bread assaulted his olfactory senses. He took a deep breath through his nose to relish the food without eating. The first person he saw was Cleveland Browns owner, Art Modell, who loved the food at Theresa's. Modell was with several guys who clearly fit the stereotype of mafioso. Who knew what they were discussing, but everybody in Cleveland knew that Modell bought the Browns on a personal shoe-string and borrowed the rest of the money. Ron wondered if some of this mob bosses had fronted him the cash.

Henry Viper and his uncle Johnny were seated in the back of the restaurant. An open bottle of red wine was on the table. They were being served fresh Italian bread with pepper and olive oil as a dipping sauce, along with olives of all shapes and sizes and colors, and some crusty parmesan cheese. Pulling his napkin away from his overgrown chin, Johnny got up and gave Ron a bear hug.

"Welcome, Ron, it's great to see you again. Just like old times."

Ron smiled slightly and recalled the horror of seeing Johnny Viper buckling his pants after screwing his mother but pretended that all was forgiven.

"Henry tells me that you're looking for work. Well, I think I have a perfect job for you. I just hired a young kid named Joey McTaggart to help run numbers and collect the dough when it's due. He's only sixteen and could use some help from a vet like you. Joey would drive the car, and both of you would collect my money together. Your cuts are 10 percent each, and that way you'll have a lot of incentive to use any means necessary when the stooge tries to back down from what he owes me. Do you get my drift, Ron?"

Ron smiled broadly and said, "Uncle Johnny, please, may I call you Uncle Johnny?"

Johnny said, "Yes, of course."

Ron gratefully replied, "Thank you, I think we have a deal."

*****

The drinks kept flowing at the Sunset Bar and Grill, and jaws were loosened as the fivesome added a po' boy sandwich to the table, along with some quesadillas for them to communally munch on.

Barb mentioned how a few years after the funeral that she finally told Jake that Michelle had been raped. He explained how his entire life had changed since then and how he had been plotting every day to avenge Michelle's rape and ultimate suicide. This caused his own life to unravel, and his tunnel vision, stirred by his love for Michelle, eventually caused Sarah to divorce him. He knew that Sarah had no choice. This compulsion made him become a horrible husband. Bruce declared that his friendship with Jake was so strong and went back so far he'd do anything to help him. Danielle brought up that she had seen a wonderful transformation in Ron over the years, and Ron began to feel like he fit in with a group of people who finally understood him. Five tropical drink-filled glasses clicked as the plan came together. They were all totally in!

Chapter 10

As the drinks continued to flow and the friends continued to imbibe, the looks on their faces turned from a collective commitment that was tying them together to a look of trepidation compounded by fear.

"Okay," said Bruce. "Yes, I'm in, but is this plan something that's going to work? Have you guys worked out all the details? Are we going to get away with murder?"

Jake answered first. "Shh, keep your voice down, Bruce. Barb and I have hashed this out for two years. Yes, we can commit the perfect crime. It helps a lot that she is one of the most skilled doctors in the country, and even more than that, she's an expert in pharmacology. When I found out from Ron that Henry was going to be on this ship, I immediately called Barb, and we both decided that this would be the perfect time and place to carry out our plan. We called you and Danielle to join us because we know how much you both had loved Michelle. It helps that the *Allure* has 6,000 passengers and almost 1,500 crew aboard, so even if the police would be suspicious about Henry's death, they'll have tons of potential suspects to question."

"But won't they find out that we were classmates and friends with Henry and thus look at us as their main suspects?" queried Danielle.

"Good point," answered Barb, "but if we do this right, the poison that we give him will be out of his system within twelve hours, and the medical examiner will conclude that Henry died of natural causes accentuated by his age, his obesity, and his drinking. We'll have committed the perfect crime!" Jake nodded in agreement, and Danielle, Bruce, and Ron finally seemed convinced.

Danielle wondered aloud, "What exactly is this poison?"

"Ricin" answered Barb. "It's been around for years, and recently some nutjobs out there have been busted for mailing it to politicians they don't like. It isn't always fatal when ingested, but when I was experimenting on some new chemotherapy drugs, I accidentally discovered an additive that makes even small doses very fatal and very quick. I'm sure the medical examiner will conclude death by heart attack, thus the perfect crime."

Danielle and Bruce seemed impressed but wondered how someone like Barb could do something that was so heinous even if it was to honor Michelle.

"Barb, isn't this against the Hippocratic oath that all doctors swear to?" asked Bruce.

"I have been living with the secret of Michelle's rape for over fifty years, having only told Jake until we let you in on the crime. If you could have seen her as she told me the details and heard her sobs, you wouldn't question my actions. I don't know how she stayed silent about that night even with the threat to her family. She kept it bottled up inside until she could stand it no more and ended her life. I must avenge her death. This plan came together accidentally in my talks with Jake. The earth will be better off with one less rapist in its midst."

Barb stunned her friends with her passionate argument to commit murder!

"Well, how do we get our hands on this chemical concoction that you've created?" asked Bruce.

"We already have it," said Jake. "I mailed it to Ron's friend Orlando last week, and he got the package yesterday. Orlando is an old army friend of Ron's who luckily happens to work in the kitchen on the *Allure*. A little money was all it took for his silence and to be persuaded to accept a package from me to give to Ron after he boarded the ship in Fort Lauderdale. It was easy to do. Barb made the pills in her lab, and she sent them to me. I put the pills into a baggie, put the baggie into a hollowed-out book, told the post office that there was nothing illegal in the package, and mailed it to Orlando on the *Allure* with a fake return address. His mail is rarely inspected nor scrutinized, and the poison is virtually undetectable anyway. Aah, the wonders of science! In other words, guys, we are in business."

*****

Nobody was surprised when Barb became a successful doctor. Her four years of premed at Ohio State were so noteworthy she had the choice of going to any medical school she wanted. She dated several interesting, young men at OSU; although she always dropped the hand of her date whenever they walked the length of the OSU quad because tradition said if you held on for the entire time and kissed your date at the end, you would eventually marry that person. Barb wanted no part of that. She went to football games in The Horseshoe, as the famous OSU stadium was nicknamed, and sometimes wandered up and down High Street in a drunken stupor; but she spent most of her time in class, in the library, in her dorms, and in the labs. Her professors often joked that she could teach their courses better than they could.

She chose to go to medical school at Harvard, where her interest in cancer research and chemotherapy blossomed. She again graduated with high honors and moved back to Cleveland to do her residency at the Cleveland Clinic, her number-one choice. Her skills, her humanity, and her overall brilliance were noticed by everyone she touched. When she finished her residency, she chose to work in the field of oncology and moonlighted as an assistant medical examiner. She thought it made a lot of sense to have one job where she helped people live as a first responder and another job where she found out why people died, thus the final responder. She reasoned that by learning about both life and death, she could help to extend the life expectancy of all mankind.

Working sixty-hour weeks and being on call once a week left Barb little time for a social life. She had dated Bruce off and on during her first year at Ohio State and his first year at Purdue and some time during their first summer back in Cleveland, but once they returned to school for their second year, their unspoken breakup became self-evident. There were no phone calls or letters to make it official, but their love for each other could not survive while they lived in quite different worlds.

Several times in their first years of college Barb did drive to Pittsburgh to visit Michelle at Carnegie Mellon. They celebrated Barb's twenty-first birthday together, but even then she could not console Michelle from the depression that haunted her daily. Barb was still the only real friend that Michelle had and now was morphing into a great doctor. But even she couldn't make Michelle laugh or smile or even inspire her to have an interest in the future. Barb never stopped worrying about her and advised that she see a psychiatrist. Michelle promised that she would think about it, but she never followed through. Oh, how things could have been different if only she had.

Barb often met Danielle for coffee at some of the trendy bistros in Cleveland Heights and in Ohio City when they were both in town. When she confided that she was really worried about Michelle, Danielle said that she was too and that they should visit her together. That never happened because Danielle was beginning to leave the closet that she had confined herself to. She was taking her art on the road, selling her paintings at galleries all around Ohio and beyond.

Barb sensed that there was something different about Danielle every time she noticed her glance at a woman the way most young men do when they see a beautiful woman walking down the street. Barb smiled as she thought Danielle might finally be finding love.

After graduating from Indiana University, Jake returned to his alma mater, JMH, and remained there for thirty-one years. He taught every type of high school history class in the curriculum and always emulated his old favorite teacher, Mr. Darbowski, who just happened to teach down the hall. Jake's first classroom was the same room 306 that he and Michelle had been assigned to for homeroom back in their freshman year of high school. He had to admit that when he walked into the room that first day as a teacher, feelings of déjà vu and dread attacked him at the same time. That day he admitted to himself that he still loved Michelle and vowed that he would try his best to discover the real cause of her rejection.

In Jake's second year of teaching, Joy Johnson, the head of the English department at JMH, introduced Jake to his future wife, Sarah Kluger. She was a first-year teacher and was new to the English department at JMH. When Jake met her for the first time, he smiled at her and was perplexed as she turned shyly away. At their first faculty party, Sarah did introduce herself to him and then introduced her good friend, Albert. She mentioned that she and Albert had a great summer travelling to England together. Jake was dismayed but tried not to show it. Later in their relationship Sarah revealed that Albert turned out to be gay. Yes, Jake knew how lucky he was by that crazy turn of events.

It was against Cleveland school policy for teachers in the same building to date each other. Jake threw caution to the wind and asked Sarah to join him at a Cleveland Browns football game. The rest is history! However, the secrecy involved in their budding love affair was something that they laughed about for years. They virtually ignored each other while at school, except for a casual hello. The caper was almost blown when Jake and Sarah's students saw them on live TV appearing on the jumbotron as they were holding hands at a Cleveland Indians game. When Sarah got to her first class the next day, their students greeted her with a sterling rendition of *Take Me Out to the Ball Game!* They decided to be up-front with their relationship and visited Principal Cihlar's office. They both breathed a sigh of relief as he told them, if they were discrete, there would be no repercussions.

In 1972 Jake married Sarah in their small apartment on the day after Thanksgiving. Their parents, siblings, six friends, and a judge

DON'T TELL A SOUL

were in attendance. They vowed not to have children for a few years, and when they did, they became the parents of twins, a boy and a girl. Sarah, whose normal top weight was about 115, ballooned up to 165 when she was pregnant. Coach Gibbons noticed her size and joked one day that there had to be two kids in there! Little did anyone know that he was right.

After his college graduation, Bruce married Marcia Roggeman, a nursing student from Michigan he had met while they were enrolled at Purdue. The newlyweds returned to Cleveland where Bruce helped to manage his father's building-supply store. Bruce and Marcia had two wonderful daughters in a five-year period, and when his father retired, Bruce ran the entire business. It thrived because of Bruce's stellar management skills and friendly personality that allowed him to sell anything to anybody.

Jake and Bruce continued their longtime friendship, which now included their wives. They could often be seen together at Indian and Browns games and helped each other move into their respective homes in suburban Lakewood, where they loved to analyze whether Nixon was a crook.

"He really is a son of a bitch," said Jake each time the topic came up.

"Nah, Jake, you're just an asshole who hates Nixon because he beat out that hippie McGovern guy," argued Bruce, but then they both laughed as they knew that nothing could destroy their friendship, not even politics.

The two young couples became regulars at the Rotary and Elks Clubs and devoted much of their time to charities and volunteer work. They became pillars of their community. They bought tickets to the Cleveland Orchestra and took in concerts at the Blossom Music Center. They were living life to its fullest.

One night, at the Red Carpet bar, after way too many drinks and without their wives, Jake and Bruce began to talk about Michelle and Barb and how great their time with them had been. They would never discuss this in front of Sarah or Marcia.

"Did you ever fuck her?" Jake asked Bruce.

"Nah, not even on prom night! Nothing really happened. Yeah, that surprised me. I thought that was going to be the night, but Barb acted weird most of that night, especially at the after-prom. And throughout that summer, I was lucky that she even kissed me. I never figured out why she was becoming so distant. And then we went off to college with barely a goodbye," responded Bruce with a tone of regret and sadness in his voice. "What about you, Jake? Did you and Michelle ever do it?"

Jake's face turned almost ashen as he answered, "No, and you know what, Bruce? I knew on prom night that something was wrong with Michelle, at least at the after-prom. That's bothered me ever since, but no matter what I've tried, I haven't found out what happened to her. I'm convinced that it was nothing that I did. But I'll tell you what, if I ever find out that someone did something to her, I will make things right because I actually still miss her a lot."

Bruce was shocked by Jake's answer, but the two of them toasted each other, as they knew they would always keep each other's secrets.

Jake kept track of Michelle through Barb. He wondered why Michelle had stayed in Pittsburgh after she graduated from Carnegie Mellon, why her plans to be a translator had never happened, why she was unemployed more than employed, and why her life was not going well at all. Whenever Jake tried to reach out to Michelle, she refused to take his call.

"The last time I saw her, she said she loved me," Jake said to Bruce while in his melancholy mood. "And now it's been seven years since I've seen her. I need to know what happened."

In their wildest dreams, Jake and Bruce would never have believed that Michelle's fate might cause them to become murderers.

When the word of Michelle's death reached Jake and Bruce, the news hit them like a missile from the sky. The obituary appeared in Cleveland's main newspaper. There was no mention of the cause of death, and little was written about a service or how friends could extend their condolences. Jake called Bruce to make sure he had read the news, and they decided to go together to Danielle's home in Ohio City, wondering if she knew any more details. Bruce picked up Jake as he figured Jake would be in no shape to drive. Barb had already left her Cleveland Heights home and was with Danielle when Jake and Bruce arrived. As the four hugged and consoled each other, it was almost like they had never been separated. Bruce, however, was uncomfortable, since he hadn't seen Barb since their sophomore year of college.

Bruce conjured up a smile, looked at her, and said, "Barb, I hear wonderful things about you and what you're doing at the Cleveland Clinic. I just want you to know that I am happy for you and applaud your success."

He meant every word of what he said and hoped that he came off as being sincere.

"Thanks so much, Bruce. I hear great things about your business as well and that you have a wonderful home with your wife and kids in Lakewood. Is it near the park?"

"Yes, it's on Kenneth Ave right on Lake Erie and less than a quarter mile from the park. It's a wonderful place for my two daughters to grow up," answered Bruce, just stating the facts.

Barb smiled as if she was genuinely happy for him.

After the small talk and catch-up ended, Jake and Bruce jumped into Bruce's Cadillac to pick up their wives while Barb and Danielle used Barb's car. They all then drove to Michelle's home on Laverne Avenue where she and Jake had frolicked as kids, where they had shared their first kiss, and where their first real love affair had begun. Philosophers and romantic writers say that it's hard to forget your first love, but it's especially difficult when the end of that relationship occurs in total mystery. What they all hoped from Michelle's parents were answers and explanations so that they could make some sense out of this horrendous event.

*****

After laying the groundwork for the ominous plan, the group left the Sunset Grill and continued their conversation back on the *Allure* in Central Park on deck 8. They sat outside on two park benches with trees swaying through the gentle breeze. Most of the passengers were sightseeing, so they had the area to themselves.

Still fearing that they would be the main suspects after they killed Henry, Bruce said, "Look, we have to do everything we can to avoid suspicion even if the death appears to be a heart attack."

"You're right," said Jake, "and Barb and I have figured out how to do that. We think the best thing to do is to welcome back Henry into our inner circle here, make him think he's our friend, and treat him like family for a few days. Let folks on the ship see how well we all get along, and then the police will never think that we could be involved in causing him any harm." Jake's answer satisfied them, but Bruce still wondered if Henry would buy the idea that the five of them could coincidentally be on the ship while he was.

"That's easy," said Barb. "We simply tell him that the four of us met Ron at our fiftieth reunion and that he had invited us to do this trip as a sort of reunion after the reunion. Then when Ron found out that Henry would also be on the ship, Ron coordinated the dates so that the reunion on the ship would be a surprise for their old class president."

"And I guess we forgot to mention that Henry hired Ron to be a detailer at one of his dealerships, so Ron and Henry were always in touch with each other," added Jake.

"But won't Henry wonder where our spouses are?" asked Bruce.

"Not really. I don't have one and neither do Barb and Danielle, so all we have to say is that Marcia would never want to stand in the way of your wish to spend time with your old friends. And besides that, we all know that Marcia gets seasick," responded Jake, who was starting to really think that yes, he and his friends just might get away with the perfect crime.

Chapter 11

Ron was the first of the conspirators to speak to Henry Viper onboard the *Allure*. The others had changed so much he would never have recognized them. Henry was sitting in the casino, betting hundred-dollar chips at the roulette table and was winning more than he was losing.

"Henry, glad you made it. You're looking good, and it looks like your bank account's doing fairly good too," said Ron with a smile on his face.

"Ron, you old motherfucker, how are you? Thanks for talking me into taking this trip. The ports are friendly, the women are stunning, and the food and service are excellent," said Henry with a slur caused by his fourth martini. "I've never taken a cruise before in my life, but now I know what I've been missing. That Viking Crown Lounge is superb, and the magician who performed at last night's show was as good a magician as I've ever seen. I'm dining at the chef's table tomorrow night. I hear it's fantastic and lasts about four hours.

Wow! This is even more fun than meeting the boys on Short Vincent Street in Cleveland back in the day. Hell, Ron, remember when Sinatra came into the Theatrical? He was a charmer. The dames were the best. Remember the Roxy, Ron, remember the broads that were there when we were young? God, we had some great times. Thanks again for suggesting this cruise."

Henry was genuinely having a great time.

"Hey, Henry, I have a surprise for you. I invited some of our old high school friends to join us on this cruise too. They're retired, still friends, and have flexible schedules, so when I told them that you and I had booked this, they arranged to come as well. They said that it would be another reunion for the best and the brightest from the class of '65."

"Well, Ron, you son of a bitch. You're always filling my life with surprises. So, tell me, who else is on board?" asked Henry.

*****

As they drove past Gunning Park near Laverne Avenue in separate cars, Jake, Bruce, Barb, and Danielle were thinking about their friendships with Michelle. Jake had loved her. Barb knew her secrets.

Danielle loved her spunk, and Bruce admired her willingness to help anyone who needed it. Michelle's death made no sense to any of them. They timed their arrivals at Michelle's parents' house to coincide so they could enter as a group. As they pulled into the driveway, none of them knew what they were going to say or do, but they knew that they had to be there together. Jake's and Bruce's wives were there to give their husbands moral support.

Jake rang the doorbell. An elderly man answered the door who introduced himself as Michelle's uncle Bob.

"Hello," said Barb. "We were friends of Michelle and wanted to extend our condolences to her parents."

"Thanks so much. Come in. Michelle's parents are in the backyard. Just go through that door," the uncle said sadly, pointing the way.

Jake led, and the friends followed into the yard. They saw Michelle's parents who were as grief-stricken as anyone they'd ever seen. When someone loses a spouse, they become a widow or widower. When someone loses their parents, they become an orphan. But there isn't a comparable word for someone who loses a child. That might be because the pain is the worst pain that anyone can ever feel.

"Mr. and Mrs. Navarre, I don't know if you remember any of us, but we went to school with Michelle and were some of her best friends. We're here to express our condolences to you and tell you that your daughter was the best. We are so saddened by what has happened," Barb was speaking for the entire group as Danielle was already in tears.

John Navarre looked at the group, embraced all of them, and said, "Thanks so much. You have no idea what your words mean to Eleanor and me. We can't believe any of this. We can't believe that she would take her own life."

John Navarre's words hit Jake, Barb, Danielle, and Bruce as if they had been crushed by a semitruck.

"Oh, we are so sorry," said Jake. "We didn't know what happened."

"Yes," said Michelle's mother, "she slit her wrists and bled to death. By the time her body was found, she had already been dead for two days. I guess nobody missed her. We talked on the phone every Sunday and had no idea that she was contemplating suicide. We both feel that we should have seen the signals." Eleanor then broke down into uncontrollable sobs.

"Barb," said John Navarre, "you just asked us if we remembered you guys. Well, of course, we do. I've never seen Michelle happier than when she was with all of you back in high school. She loved being with all of you, and Jake, she loved you the most. I think she was fully prepared to follow you anywhere once she graduated from college. I think she wanted to marry you and give you children. But that summer after high school, things changed. Jake, Eleanor, and I never knew what happened, but we always had our suspicions. We need you to tell us what happened between you and Michelle. Why did you break up? And I need to know if you hurt our daughter?"

At this point, John Navarre was sobbing and yelling at the same time. Jake was afraid. He never gave it a thought that he could be the reason for Michelle's death.

But Bruce intervened strongly, "Mr. and Mrs. Navarre, we all loved Michelle, and Jake loved her more than anyone. We never knew what happened to cause her melancholy, but we know that she somehow changed, and that change happened on prom night. I promise you that Jake had nothing to do with it. He noticed the change in her as well. Both of us reached out to Michelle after she left for college early. That made no sense to any of us, and Jake went to visit her and wrote her letters and called her on the phone, but she never confided in him. She broke it off when she felt that he was too persistent in trying to find the truth. Jake was heartbroken when that happened. I swear to God, Mr. and Mrs. Navarre, we have no idea what happened either."

Bruce's words were coming from his heart, and Mr. and Mrs. Navarre knew that. They embraced Jake, Bruce, Barb, and Danielle, and they all cried together. Barb didn't talk at all. Instead, a voice in her head kept telling her not to break the promise she had made to Michelle. Sarah and Marcia watched from afar, and Sarah wondered if Jake loved her now as much as he had loved Michelle.

At that time, the Catholic church would not hold funerals for the victims of a suicide. Michelle Navarre had been a member of Our Lady of Angels Parish on Rocky River Drive. When her parents tried to get Father Burke to waive the rule, the good father said that if he did, the bishop would have his head and report him to the Vatican. John Navarre wondered how Holy Rosary Parish could give a full church send-off to the murdering gangsters who died on Murray Hill, but the Catholic Church viewed suicide victims as being unworthy of a proper burial by the church. Didn't they deserve the same treatment as a lousy murderer received? Eleanor exclaimed her unhappiness to Father Burke that included more profanity then she had ever spoken in her lifetime. Father Burke blamed it on her grief. Eleanor never saw Father Burke again.

Eleanor and John Navarre had arranged a memorial service for Michelle at the Chambers Funeral Home on Rocky River Drive. A hearse returned the body from Pittsburgh to Cleveland. Her parents decided that Michelle deserved a closed casket because the morticians at Chambers said that they could not work miracles with a body that had been undiscovered for two days. Eleanor and John agreed but asked to get a look at the body before the service. They hardly recognized their daughter and cried together for what felt like an eternity.

Michelle's service was attended by hundreds of her classmates from Marshall and by everyone who knew her in the West Park neighborhood. The service encouraged anyone who wanted to speak about Michelle to do so. Funny stories were told, as were stories about her ability to learn and speak languages. Those who didn't know Michelle very well learned how wonderful she was. Many of her teachers attended said that they would never forget her and how extraordinary a student she had been. And then it was Jake's turn to speak.

Jake had never spoken at a funeral, and as he left his seat next to his wife, every nerve in his body was tingling, and sweat was covering every pore as if he had just run a marathon.

"Good morning, everyone. My name is Jake Markowski. I met Michelle when we were in the sixth grade, and yes, she soon became my best friend. We had so much fun together. We grew up together. We laughed, and we even cried together, especially when we were watching a sad movie. Michelle was special. Not only was she beautiful but she was the smartest girl that I ever went to school with, and gosh, when she asked me to dance with her for the first time way back in sixth grade, I felt like she really liked me. I had hit the jackpot. I knew I already liked her more than I could possibly tell her. It's hard to say I love you when you are so young, but I knew that my feelings were more than a crush. I loved it when she spoke to me with a French accent or when she spoke any language that sounded exotic." Jake paused as he could feel the tears building inside of him. "But then after high school, we broke up. That happens a lot in life. It's probably happened to many of you in this room. When it happens, you try to pick up the pieces and you move on. So I moved on. I was so lucky to meet my wife, Sarah, and fall in love again. Michelle's death is illogical. It's senseless," Jake stated with his voice rising. "There must be something behind it that none of us knows or understands. Hopefully, someone can help us get to the bottom of her unnecessary death. I will miss her tremendously."

As Jake returned to his seat, he noticed that most of the mourners were dabbing their tear-stained eyes, but his wife, Sarah, did not meet his gaze. Even Ron Bloodstone and Pat Torrence were crying like third graders who had their lunch money taken by the class bully. Michelle's parents shook Jake's hand and embraced him, and old classmates patted Jake on the back and congratulated him on his wonderful eulogy. Ron Bloodstone and Henry Viper were the last two mourners to leave the funeral home.

In front of the closed casket, they both uttered some prayers, and then Henry whispered to Ron, "She was the best piece of ass I ever had."

Ron was stunned!

A family reception was held for the mourners at Tony's Diner. More stories were revealed, and old times at Marshall were shared with classmates who had not seen each other in years. Even the teachers seemed humanized to many from the class of '65 who had feared them when they were students. Mr. Darbowski even gave a glowing tribute, calling Michelle one of the best students he had in his long career. After the drinks had filled everybody to the point of insobriety, and the food had forced the men to increase their belt size, everyone left and hoped that they would get together in happier times. John and Eleanor Navarre cried for a long, long time.

Sarah Markowski was not among the people who congratulated Jake for his eulogy. In fact, she ignored him for the rest of the day.

She had a look of concern and even fear on her face, and when she finally talked to Jake as they were driving home from the funeral, she said, "I never knew you had those feelings for Michelle. I knew that she was your old girlfriend, but Jake, but I don't think you ever got over her. Do you still love me?"

*****

Ron had arranged to take Henry to the Rising Tide to meet his old classmates. After his late night at the casino, a hungover and now re-intoxicated Henry did not appreciate the bar rising like an open elevator.

"Son of a bitch, is it Jake Markowski? And damn, is that you, Bruce Goodman? And who are these lovely ladies with you? Are they your wives?" slurred Henry when he entered the bar.

"Well, damn, Henry, aren't you a sight for sore eyes!" said Jake through gritted teeth as he met Michelle's rapist. "And no, I'm not married. This is Barb Moody, or should I say Doctor Barb Moody. Do you remember her? She was our class brainiac. Our 'most likely to succeed,' and succeed she did. And this here is Danielle Stevens. They were both in our class, and you know what, I bet they both voted for you when you ran for senior-class president."

They all laughed; although it was a forced laugh for all except Henry.

Bruce said, "Henry, great to see you again, and no, my wife, Marcia, is not with me. She suffers from seasickness and decided that after fifty years of marriage that she could trust me to go on a fun trip alone. It's really good to see you again."

The night went better than the partners in crime ever imagined. Henry told a lot of stories about his old days in Cleveland, including his time as a gangster, a pimp, and a con man. He talked about the time he had spent in jail for murdering a rival gang leader and lauded his uncle Johnny for getting him out after only serving two years. He talked openly about his days on Murray Hill and how he still loved Theresa's great Italian restaurant. He brought up the councilmen who accepted his bribes and the mayors who covered up crimes after they drank his liquor at his mansion. He bragged about all the women that he had known and screwed, as had his friends from the Cleveland Browns.

Henry's tone changed as he explained how he had reformed his life once he was released from jail. With the help of his family, Henry moved into the business of selling cars in Cleveland. His small Ford/Lincoln dealership grew quickly, and before he was fifty, Henry was running five dealerships in the Cleveland area. Helped by his tacky, commercials on local TV that promised perspective buyers the best deal ever on a car, Henry had become legitimate and more success-ful than he ever was as a gangster. Yes, Henry had become likeable, something that bothered the friends with him at the bar. Maybe he really was a reformed man who deserved forgiveness.

Chapter 12

Henry was the first of them to leave the Rising Tide after the night of fun, debauchery, and reminiscing. He returned to his cabin, had a nightcap from the minibar in his suite, and as he turned in, he began to wonder if what he had just enjoyed was real or if there was something else going on behind the scenes that he couldn't comprehend. *They hated me in high school,* he thought to himself, *and after high school, they made conscious efforts to avoid me, especially when I became a successful car salesman. Why are they being so nice to me now?* As Henry lapsed into a deep, drunken sleep, he hoped that his old friends were just letting bygones be bygones. But he wasn't exactly sure and smiled when he remembered the advice of a young Michael Corleone from *The Godfather* who once said, "Keep your friends close and your enemies closer."

After Henry left the bar for the night, Danielle was the first to speak.

"I hate to say this, but he seemed to be a nice guy tonight. When he asked me how my painting was going and when he congratulated me for my new life in LA, he seemed genuinely interested and happy for me. I didn't expect any of that."

"He acted like someone who's changed for the better," Bruce chimed in. "I can't believe that this is someone whose past life was horrific. But we all know what he did. I hate to admit it, but part of me liked the new Henry a lot."

"Bruce, he raped Michelle. He ruined her life," yelled Barb in a voice that was heard by three or four drunks who were still toasting away the night while compounding their own personal miseries. "We can't forget that."

Danielle and Bruce had never seen Barb so passionate about anything, but both were having doubts about why they were there, and Jake and Barb both sensed it.

Jake knew that he had to intervene.

"Listen, everyone, we've all invested time, money, and energy into this trip. Second-guessing is a natural thing. But please remember Michelle. Remember how great she was. Remember how we all loved her. And never forget what Henry did to her. We cannot wash his sins away."

Throughout the evening Ron had been quieter than anyone. He was storing the poison in his safe in his stateroom. They only had five more days on the ship and wanted all this to end quickly. He was already wondering if somebody might discover the ricin. It wasn't too hard to get into anyone's safe on the ship. You just had to know the right folks, and Ron knew the right folks. He had been saved by cruise ships and worked on them for ten years during his bout with PTSD in his post-Vietnam years. The Veterans Administration had not helped. Women he dated just thought he was a loser. Even Henry had cast aspersions on him when Ron asked for help. So, after working for Henry in the rackets, and after watching Henry get sent to jail, Ron ran away. He became homeless. He worked odd jobs. He begged on street corners. He walked into church sanctuaries to pray and asked God for help. The help came when he saw an advertisement from Royal Caribbean Cruise Line for help needed in their kitchens. He cleaned himself up, applied for the job, and landed it. Getting that job had saved Ron. He appreciated what the cruise line had done for him. His travels on the ships and the friendships he made, especially with the cabin stewards, bartenders, and waiters had been the best therapy that he had since his return from 'Nam. After working on the seas for ten years, Ron returned to Cleveland as a new man. And when Henry offered him a job as the detail manager at one of his dealerships, he felt honored to accept it from a man who had also turned his life around seemingly for the better.

But no matter how hard Ron worked and no matter how impressed he was by his boss's turn-around, he still could not live knowing that Henry had raped Michelle leading to her eventual death. Was that ever going to stop bothering him? As he now sat in his cabin, wondering if somebody might discover the ricin, Ron was extremely conflicted. On one hand, killing Henry was justified to avenge Michelle's rape and subsequent suicide. But on the other hand, if Henry had reformed and was sorry for his sins, could he participate in Henry's murder? Ron couldn't honestly answer that question.

*****

On the way home from Michelle's funeral, Sarah asked Jake if he still loved her.

He blurted out, "Of course, I do, Sarah. You're wonderful. You're the best mother to our kids, my best friend, and I could not live without you."

As Jake said those words, he was sincere, but he sensed that Sarah didn't believe him. She knew that his eulogy at the funeral was his public revelation that Michelle was his true love. He wondered how he could have been so stupid as to say those words in public. He knew that his words had embarrassed and humiliated Sarah. His passion for Michelle was obvious, and now his marriage might be in trouble. Although it would be ten more years before Jake and Sarah divorced, their relationship was never the same after Michelle's death.

Five years after the funeral, Jake got a call from Barb.

"I've got to see you," she said. "Let's meet for drinks at the Grog Shop downtown tomorrow around seven p.m."

Barb and Jake had hardly seen each other over those five years. Barb was growing her career at the Cleveland Clinic and began to win accolades for her work in cancer research, especially in the area of safe and effective chemotherapy drugs that lessened the hair loss that commonly occurred in the therapy. Jake taught his history classes six times a day in a monotone without the passion that once made him a great teacher. He was working on his marriage, and since Sarah wasn't ready to see a marriage counselor, Jake decided the best way to win her back was to become the best father possible. His kids became the focus of his life. Nothing else mattered more to him. When he tore the meniscus in his right knee during a pickup basketball game, he required surgery. This scared his kids who watched as Sarah, the dutiful wife, helped him recover. He knew then that he totally loved his life and children, but it was obvious that Sarah was only going through the motions. A divorce was imminent. It would crush his kids, and he desperately didn't want his marriage to end.

As Jake entered the Grog Shop right at 7:00, he saw Barb huddled in a back booth in the bar. Even though happy hour was in full swing, she'd found a quiet place to sit and talk.

Michael Jackson's song, *Billie Jean,* was being blasted throughout the bar, and when Jake saw Barb, he quipped, "Certainly better than disco!" When Barb didn't laugh at Jake's warped joke, he immediately sensed that she had something important on her mind. "How are you, Barb?" Jake said as he hugged her tightly as if she was his best longtime friend.

"Jake, I'm so sorry that I've put you on the outs over the last few years. I miss you and Bruce and Sarah and Marcia. If you haven't heard, Danielle has moved to LA. I used to hang with her a lot, but now she's gone. I miss all of you. Sometimes life just gets in the way of things that really matter. I need to learn that lesson. I am devoured by my work. It makes me happy, but I know that work is just a distraction for me. It's a cover-up for things that are bothering me. It's a veil for my loneliness. All that needs to change. Jake, we're in our thirties now. I need to live my life. I need to unburden myself from the secrets that I've been carrying. I need to have friends that I can enjoy and trust. And I want to tell you what I've been keeping from you for all these years."

As her words came out, Barb burst into tears. Her mascara was running down her face, and she looked to Jake as if age was consuming her long before it should have.

"Barb, what's wrong? What the hell is going on? What do you want to tell me?" Jake softly whispered as he tried his best to console her.

As her sobbing began to subside, Barb said, "I've been keeping this secret for over fifteen years. I promised that I would keep it forever. But things have changed, and I can't hold it inside any longer. Jake, it's driving me crazy. I'm a wreck. The secret has infected my life, and I need to get back to living."

"Barb, please tell me," urged Jake, whose own feelings were beginning to come apart at the seams as he had no clue what Barb was talking about.

Through her sniffles and countless tears, Barb detailed to Jake what happened to Michelle the night of their high school prom. She had never forgotten the words that Michelle had shared with her. She had never forgotten the look of fear on Michelle's face, and she had not been able to live with herself since Michelle's death. The guilt was eating her alive.

"I should have told somebody," she said through the tears. "She would be alive today had I called the police and reported her rape, but I didn't do it. She would be alive today if it weren't for me. I'm to blame for Michelle's death. Jake, her attacker told her that he would kill her family if she ever told a soul."

Jake began to shake with rage. He grabbed Barb's arms and pulled her forcefully out of her seat.

"Is everything okay, sir?" asked one of the waitresses.

"Yes," said Jake through his heavy breathing. "She just needs a breath of fresh air. I'm taking her outside. Thanks for your concern."

"What the fuck, Barb! How could you not tell me?" yelled Jake as they got outside. He was feeling a rage he had never felt before. "I loved her, Barb. I would've helped her. I would've called the police. I could have caught the son of a bitch. If you had only told me,

Michelle would be alive today! Her death is on you," he screamed. "Barb, why didn't you tell me?"

As these words stormed out of Jake's mouth, tears filled his eyes. He yelled out as if he was in unbearable pain, and then he collapsed to the ground.

Jake laid limp on the edge of the dusty street. He felt as if his soul had been released from his body. He felt betrayed and that all was lost. Then he felt Barb's embrace. She was holding him as tightly as he had ever been held. He felt her tears flowing freely on his face and heard her uncontrollable sobs. And then he remembered that Barb had said the rapist would kill Michelle's family if the incident was reported. Only then did Jake understand.

Jake and Barb walked seemingly forever throughout downtown Cleveland and did not notice another person as they cried and tried to comfort each other. He didn't know what to say to Barb. How could he? He felt her pain. He understood her guilt, and he was happy that she finally trusted him with the truth. When they reached Public Square, they found a bench in front of the Old Stone Church and embraced each other again as they sat down. They had both finally calmed down.

"I appreciate that you finally trusted me enough to share the truth," said Jake in a soft voice that was barely more than a whisper. "Yes, it was more than puppy love, Barb. I really loved Michelle and felt that we would have had a great future had we been allowed to. I miss her always, and ever since her death, I hurt more every day as I search for answers to why she committed suicide. Thanks for giving me the answer to all that. The question of what happened between Michelle and I was eating me alive."

"I know all that," said Barb once her tears dried up. "She asked me to not tell a soul, so I had to keep my word. It was the hardest thing that I've ever done, but I now realize that it might have been the biggest mistake I've ever made too."

"Barb, you know that I have to ask you this. Who raped her? Did she tell you? Do you know who it is?" questioned Jake.

"He was disguised, but Michelle did say that she may have recognized his voice, but no, she never told me who she thought it might be. She wanted to go on about her life as if nothing had happened. I agreed to keep her secret and pretend that things were fine. She just wanted to move on," said Barb.

"But Barb," exclaimed Jake, "if she thought she recognized the voice, then the guy was somebody that she knew. He might have been one of our classmates."

"I've thought that since the prom and have played amateur detective, trying to think about our classmates and who could have done this."

"And do you have a suspect?" interrupted Jake.

"No," said Barb, "and that's driving me crazy."

As they left the park bench, Jake looked into Barb's eyes and saw both the pain and the relief that she was feeling because she had finally revealed her long-held secret. Jake returned home and had to explain to Sarah why he was so late. He merely said that he had some business to take care of, knowing fully well that he couldn't share the truth with Sarah about Barb's sobbing revelation. The idea that someone had raped Michelle would cause him pain forever.

Barb returned to her large Cleveland Heights home alone with her fears but with the hope that things might change for the better in her life now that she had unburdened her soul. She knew that she had to help Jake find the rapist.

*****

The Windjammer buffet was the default place where everyone ate breakfast on the *Allure*. Every conceivable type of food was served, the service was top-shelf, and that's where Ron joined Bruce and Jake for breakfast the morning after they all met up with Henry Viper.

"Good morning, gentlemen," said Ron. "We had quite a night last night, didn't we? Even my feet are hungover this morning." They all laughed at the joke. "So what do you guys think? The longer we drag this out, the more chance we have of something going wrong. We need to finalize the plan and act soon."

Jake agreed, but Bruce fired back with his increasing nervousness and his growing reluctance, saying that he needed assurance that their plan was foolproof. And he even admitted again that Henry might be a reformed man.

"Bruce," said Jake, "that might be true, but he needs to pay for what he did to Michelle."

Bruce reluctantly agreed, as he was still uncertain if he could go through with any of this.

Danielle arrived in the Windjammer and beheld in the buffet the seemingly twenty different ways that eggs could be cooked, not to mention the made-to-order chef. Just as she decided that an omelet with ham, cheese, mushrooms, and green onions was her customized choice, Barb came up behind her. They made small talk as she put in her egg choice, two eggs over easy.

With their freshly cooked breakfast choices in hand, the two women joined the guys at a secluded table by the window. With this vantage point, they were able to watch the ship dock in Saint Thomas, another beautiful, tropical island. So far, each port seemed better than the last.

As they were finishing their repast, Jake said, "Hey, ladies, we've decided that we'll finish the job the day after tomorrow, the second day we're docked in Aruba. Speak your piece right now if you disagree."

With strained faces, nobody uttered a word.

Chapter 13

As the nerves began to tingle more and more among the conspirators, they disembarked at their second port of call, Saint Thomas in the US Virgin Islands. The group had already discussed which island to commit the dirty deed. Because it was a US possession, Saint Thomas was ruled out as the place to kill Henry.

"Too much technology that might detect us," Bruce had suggested.

"And they have a police force skilled in US methods," added Ron, who didn't let on whether that was knowledge from personal experience.

Barb had reminded them that where the ship was on the high seas was irrelevant, as was the flag that they're flying.

"If either the suspects or the victims are US nationals and the ship has left or is going to a US port, then the FBI has full juris-diction in any case. Ships don't have their own police force. Most important is where the ship is based. Royal Caribbean is based in Miami, so yes, the FBI would investigate."

The group walked around the port but found not even the gorgeous scenery and swaying palm trees could keep their minds off what they were about to do. They were all thinking the same thing. They had to do this awful deed, but how would they survive in prison if they got caught? How would doing this impact their reputations and their families? They had all worked hard to make a positive impact in life. Even Ron had turned things around. As they mulled this over in their own heads, they each were thinking the same thing: *Don't tell a soul that I did this, and please don't let my friends know that I wanted to back out.*

*****

The deterioration in Jake and Sarah's marriage was slow and painful for both. After Michelle's funeral, Jake remained a great father but was a husband who seemed miles away from his wife even though he was physically present. When they were secretly dating while being teachers at the same building, the secret liaisons they had where they would sneak into closets and maul each other in the middle of the school day had now morphed into ignoring each other when they passed in the halls of JMH. They ate their lunches with other teachers instead of each other.

At home they tried to put on a good face for their children. Holidays were special for the kids but became joyless for the two of them. Spring-break vacations found the couple going their separate ways as Sarah visited museums and took tours alone while Jake and his twins frolicked on the beach. All attempts at sex, better communication, and seeking some form of reconciliation were discarded by both as their coldness toward each other grew. Neither of them wanted to pursue counseling. When the twins turned thirteen, Jake and Sarah moved into separate bedrooms. Their kids asked them why. Neither were convincing with their idiotic answers, and both Jake and Sarah knew that their kids were on to them and that their marriage was finally over.

As things fell apart at home, Jake spent more time with Bruce than he did with Sarah.

As they were drinking one day at the Red Carpet, something that was becoming almost a daily occurrence, Bruce said, "Hey, buddy, what's wrong?"

He knew that Jake needed to talk but that he wouldn't be cogent if he drank a third Manhattan.

"I've lost her, Bruce. I've lost Sarah, and I don't know what to do or how to fix this," lamented Jake as the tears began to flow from his eyes. "The worst thing is that my kids sense it and are wondering what's wrong and are asking if we're getting a divorce."

"Do you still love Sarah, Jake? Have you tried everything in your power to talk to her about counseling?" offered Bruce. "Would it help if I asked Marcia to have a talk with Sarah? You know how women are with each other and how close the two of them are. Maybe Marcia's suggestion for counseling would work."

"That might help, but Sarah will most likely refuse. She believes that I never loved her as much as I loved Michelle and that she can't compete with that love even though Michelle is dead. I've thought of having private counseling, but it would be a waste of money because I already know the truth. If I went to a shrink, I would have admitted that Michelle was the love of my life and that nobody else could match that love. Yes, I once loved Sarah, but never as much as I loved Michelle. And now I have to do whatever I can to make things right."

Jake and Sarah's divorce settlement was a quick no-fault agreement where the couple split their assets and agreed to have joint custody of their children. Jake got them on weekends and alternate holidays, and Sarah kept them on weekdays. Sarah kept the house, and Jake moved into a small apartment in Lakewood, close enough that the kids would easily walk. He worked part-time jobs to save money for his kid's college fund and often felt like he was negligent in not having the money to provide for them in the way that they deserved. After all, he and Sarah had done this to them. The kids were not at fault, and yet their lives were being torn apart. The guilt that burdened Jake never disappeared, even after his kids grew to adulthood. He always felt that Sarah was blameless in the divorce and hoped that she didn't feel the overbearing sadness that he did.

Sarah once loved Jake more than she ever thought she could love anyone. She had grown up in Cleveland, much like Jake did, and had gone to James Ford Rhodes High School in the Old Brooklyn neighborhood of Cleveland. Ironically, Sarah had been a cheerleader for Rhodes and cheered them to many victories over rival, John Marshall High School, when Jake was a student there. She graduated from Kent State in 1970 and was there on May 4 when the shots were fired by the Ohio National Guard that killed four students who happened to be in the wrong place at the wrong time. One victim, Bill Schroeder, a member of his high school junior ROTC, had been one of Sarah's friends. Bill had graduated from Lorain High School twenty-five miles west of Cleveland, something that tethered Bill and Sarah at Kent.

That incident changed Sarah forever. Although not technically a left-wing-leaning, pot-smoking, commune-living hippie as many of her classmates were, Sarah developed a social consciousness after the shooting that changed her life. She was into supporting good causes, challenging authority, and speaking her mind when she felt she was in the right. She knew good from evil, and when she met Jake, she discovered quickly that he was like-minded.

Sarah was attracted to Jake almost immediately. They were introduced at an opening of the school year by Joy Johnson, the English department chairman. Jake was now a second-year teacher, and Sarah was a rookie who had just spent her summer travelling to England with Albert Morningstar, a Kent grad student who was trying to write a romantic novel after failing to become a romantic poet. Sarah had to get away from the chaos that ensued after the Kent shootings. That event had changed her life to the point that she hated violence, hated guns, hated war, and was questioning her own career choice. "How was being an English teacher going to help make the world a better place?" became a mantra that spun through her head.

Albert was not really her boyfriend but was an interesting-enough guy, a true romantic; and when he asked her to travel with him to England, she agreed to go on a wonderful adventure before she began the rigors of being a first-year teacher.

When Sarah was first introduced to Jake, Joy mentioned that Sarah had just travelled throughout England with her boyfriend to study the English romantic poets and how that trip would help Sarah become a great teacher. Jake later told her that when he heard the word "boyfriend," he immediately thought that she was unavailable. Little did he know at the time that Sarah was smitten with him right at that first introduction and that she later asked Joy to refrain from saying that she had a boyfriend. Love at first sight!

During Sarah's first year of teaching, Jake was always there for her, giving his ideas on the tricks of the trade that might make some-one a good teacher. He even helped her and her roommate, Stephanie Clarke, move into a new apartment.

At the pizza party thrown by the girls to pay back the folks who helped them move, Stephanie, although very tipsy, cornered Jake and said, "Jake, what the hell is wrong with you? Why aren't you going after Sarah? She's infatuated with you. Open your eyes!" She later relayed her conversation to Sarah. Jake had thought that Albert was

Sarah's boyfriend, and thus he didn't pursue her. Stephanie set him straight, "Jake, I thought you knew. Albert's gay. Sarah found this out about a month ago. I figured she told you already, but I bet she was too embarrassed. You should go after her. She really likes you and has been waiting a year for you to show some interest."

Sarah was thrilled when he called her that very night and asked her to go with him to the Browns/Patriots football game. It was a great first date buoyed by the fact that the Browns were the victors!

The Cleveland school system had a strict policy that forbade teachers who worked in the same building from dating each other, so two lovebirds spent a lot of time in the corners of dark bars and restaurants, trying to be as inconspicuous as possible. If they were discovered, one or both would be transferred to other schools in the system, and neither of them wanted that. Sarah thought it was fun for them to see each other almost 24-7 as they passed in the hallways and spent downtime in the teachers' lounges. With their low, young-teacher salaries, it soon became cost-effective for Jake to move into Sarah's apartment. He convinced her that it would be great to split the rent since her roommate had married and moved out. What a great way for two lowly paid teachers to save some money and have their own little love nest. She could not have been happier!

After Jake moved in with Sarah, discretion became a bigger issue since the school board said that living together was fine for members of the same sex, but not for members of the opposite sex. What would happen if they were caught? What would happen when the school board noticed that they were using the same address? They wondered how the teachers who were gay and living together got away with breaking that rule. "Perhaps the school board stupidly believes that nobody's gay," said Jake as they both laughed at the stupidity of the work rules and the ridiculousness of the stodgy policies that took away their individual freedoms.

After six months of cohabitation, Jake and Sarah got married. She loved their small, intimate wedding that took place in their apartment and included their parents, siblings, and six friends as the honored guests and witnesses. Jake invited Gary and Sherman, his college roommates, along with Bruce Goodman; and Sarah tapped Stephanie, along with two of her coworkers at Marshall to attend. It was a top-secret wedding that took place over Thanksgiving break. The ceremony was performed by Judge Burt Pilarski, who at the time was the youngest judge in Cuyahoga County. Ironically, Pilarski ended up in jail himself for abusing his wife; but luckily, he wasn't arrested for his crime until after their wedding ceremony.

When the newly married couple walked into JMH on the Monday after Thanksgiving, they strolled nonchalantly into the teachers' lounge where the coffee was stronger than ever and proudly announced the news.

"Guess what, guys? Sarah and I got married over the weekend. You're the first to know!" Jake proudly stated with his happiest voice.

"What'd you do, knock her up?" yelled coach Gibbons as everybody laughed.

"Who's going to be the one to get transferred out of here when the board finds out?" teased Bill Fox, the football coach. "God, I hope it's you, Jake. Sarah's much easier on my old eyes than you are," he continued as everyone laughed.

But despite their sins, it was obvious that everybody on the staff was giving them their full blessings and support. Sarah was relieved that their fellow teachers were happy for them. That was verified by the end of the day when Principal Cihlar called Jake and Sarah into his office, congratulated them on their marriage, and told them that if they did not do any unnecessary fraternization during the day, their jobs would be fine.

"It really is a stupid rule," said Cihlar as Jake and Sarah grinned from ear to ear.

DON'T TELL A SOUL

Sarah's happiness was at a peak at that moment, but like many things in life, it began to decay as time moved along, and life intervened into their wedded bliss.

*****

As the friends walked back to the port in Saint Thomas, the plan on how to kill Henry Viper was finalized. Ron would separate the invigorated, nondetectable ricin into five parts, and each part would be put into a small plastic container that was made of solid black plastic and would be covered with a tight lid. The container looked like a single serving of coffee creamer that you would find in a restaurant or a coffee pod that you might use in a Keurig coffeepot. Ron would keep one of the pods for himself and would give one each to Jake, Barb, Danielle, and Bruce.

At dinner two days from now, once the ship was back at sea after departing from Aruba, everyone's job was to make the best of any opportunity they had to distract Henry so that one of them could easily open their container and pour the poison into Henry's food or drink. If someone could get him to leave the room for a minute or if he went to the bathroom on his own, all the better. And if more than one of them got to place the poison into Henry's food or drink, they could rationalize that it was somebody else's poison, not theirs, that killed Henry. It all seemed too easy. Would it work? Could they turn the evening into one where no one seemed nervous, and none of them would be under suspicion when the body was found? They would all need their best poker faces and would have to be as normal as possible. Could they do it? Or might their second thoughts sabotage the plan? They figured that carrying out their plan as the ship was leaving Aruba, having been docked for two days, would be the best time to act. In the meantime, they drank, they walked, they gambled and tried to have fun, but none of that eased their nerves that were coming unglued.

Chapter 14

The port at Aruba was often the highlight for many of the folks who sailed in the Southern Caribbean. Filled with hotspots, beautiful scenery of every type imaginable, plus people of over one hundred nationalities, this constituent country of the Netherlands is the melting pot that the United States aspires to be. It's a haven for the rich and famous and is considered safe, very European, and best of all for many, it's outside the Caribbean hurricane alley. When the *Allure* docked at Oranjestad, almost every passenger left the ship to go ashore. Those who stayed onboard loved the chance to use the hot tubs alone and to eat in facilities without crowds of people near them.

Aruba was wonderful. Some visitors rented scooters. Others took historical excursions to learn why the Dutch loved the place, and others went to the western part of the island to discover the sand dunes that looked so much like Arizona folks imagined seeing Gene Autry riding into the sunset.

Henry Viper was one of the first passengers off the ship. He jumped into a cab and headed for the Eagle Aruba Casino to scratch his gambling itch that couldn't be completely scratched on the ship because the *Allure* frowned on high rollers. Henry wanted to bet a lot more than the meager amount *Allure* allowed. His successful car dealerships made it possible for him to lose $100 a spin on the roulette wheel or $100 a game at the blackjack table without blinking an eye or feeling the pain of the loss. He loved the action, and most of the time he won much more than he lost. By 10:00 a.m. Henry was up almost $5,000 and was having a blast. When he played the number 17 on the wheel, and it hit, he screamed out, "Thanks, Cleveland, you've been really good to me."

"Are you from Cleveland?" said a voice coming from a young man seated right next to Henry.

"Yes, the West Park neighborhood, but most recently from Murray Hill. Hello, young man, my name is Henry Viper."

The young man smiled and said, "Hi, Henry, I am Tommy Torino. I grew up on the east side, in the Collinwood area, but yeah, I love the Murray Hill area too. Great restaurants there. I'm here on my honeymoon."

"Aah, you must be taking a break from the new Mrs. I bet she's busting your balls," said Henry with a big smile on his face."

"Damn, I never knew that marriage could be this demanding," laughed Tommy. "She's tiring me out. Hell, I'm only twenty-five, and I'm already wondering if I'll still have the energy to fuck by the time I'm thirty. I'm scoping out things to do in Aruba while she rests up for our next round!" responded Tommy as both began to roar and act as if they'd been lifelong friends. "Hey, Henry, are you the guy that does those wacky car commercials that I see on TV, *that* Henry Viper?" asked Tommy.

"At your service, young man, that's me. It's nice to meet someone from Cleveland. Let me buy you a drink," said Henry as the two walked over to the bar.

It was customary for Henry to drink a lot, but to his credit, he usually waited until at least 3:00 p.m. to start imbibing, but he was going to make an exception today. He was having a great time on the cruise. He connected with some old high school friends and had won the *Allure's* famous belly flop contest that caused him to blush when the crowd gave him a standing ovation, and at almost three hundred pounds, Henry had a lot of blush to show! Now he felt like he could be a Yoda to his new young friend. Tommy, on the other hand, was

JIM WASOWSKI & CONNIE FRIESS

not much of a drinker, but he'd always been told to respect his elders and felt that his new bride would forgive him if he sat and had a few drinks with Henry. After all, in the mind of Tommy, Henry was a successful Cleveland icon, and it would be disrespectful if he turned down a free drink. His grandpa had always taught him to respect his elders.

As the day ran into the early afternoon, Henry and Tommy discussed the Tribe and their run in the 2016 World Series. They agreed that it was a great Series and that star pitcher, Corey Kluber, had let them down. They talked about the parade that celebrated the Cavaliers' championship and wondered how long Lebron James would remain on the team. They agreed that Cleveland needed the Browns to become a contender again to solidify the people of the city that were craving for a Super Bowl appearance by their longtime heroes. Then the talk turned in a totally new direction.

"Hey, Tommy," said Henry as he was carefully choosing his words. "I was just wondering if you might be related to an old friend of mine who had your same last name. He was a goombah named Frankie Torino. He grew up around Murray Hill and played a little football himself at John Hay High School. I worked with him for a while when I was a kid. We both drove cars for my uncle Johnny

Viper and had a lot of fun together. God, sometimes I miss those days," whispered Henry. "I even went to Frankie's wedding. Frankie had a wonderful wife. I don't remember her name, but I do remember that she once wore a beautiful blue dress with a sapphire necklace that matched her gorgeous blue eyes. God, she sparkled in that dress and necklace. She was beautiful," said Henry, with a nostalgic expression on his face. His mood went from one of being uplifting and boisterous to one of quietness and even regret.

"Well, Mr. Viper, there are many Torinos in Murray Hill, but my grandfather is named Frankie," said Tommy. "He could be your old friend, but I would have no way of knowing. I am not that old, you know."

They both laughed as Henry bought them a final round.

The new friends finished their drinks and rose from their bar stools.

"See you around, kid. I'll be back here tomorrow morning first thing to win a little more money before the ship sets sail for home tomorrow night. Come join me and bring that new bride of yours. I'd love to see who you're fucking," Henry shouted a bit loudly, liquor the cause of his slurred and boisterous voice. They both laughed.

"See you tomorrow, Mr. Viper," said Tommy. "I'll bring Sophia, and I want to buy you lunch. How about noon at Passions on the Beach? It's right next door to the casino."

He knew how to show respect for his elders, especially those as famous as Henry Viper. They waved goodbye as Tommy walked away, agreeing to meet tomorrow.

Tommy returned to his stateroom, a beautiful balcony suite, which was paid for by his grandpa. Even though his new bride, Sophia, was angry that she had awakened without her husband, she quickly calmed down when Tommy told her about his time onshore and who he had met.

"God, that Henry is a loudmouth on TV. His commercials are so bad they're funny, but I know they must help him sell a lot of cars," Sophia said.

"He's not a bad guy at all," added Tommy. "He probably drinks too much, but he seems to be the sort of guy that would do anything for his friends. I think I'll call my grandfather and tell him who I bumped into."

Frankie Torino was now seventy-one years of age and still vital for a man of that age. He never missed mass at Holy Rosary, donated to every building fund, and was always one of the proud dignitaries at the feast of the Assumption. His life had been filled with controversy, scandals, and prison time, but he had been a respectable citizen for over twenty years.

"Grandpa, it's me, Tommy," he eagerly said over the phone.

"Oh my god, is everything okay? I can't believe that you would call your grandpa in the middle of your honeymoon," exclaimed Frankie. "Are you enjoying that suite that I got you? I think I told you I had connections to get you the best cabin on the ship."

"Things are going great, Grandpa. The cruise is fantastic, the cabin is the best, the food is awesome, and Sophia is wonderful. I married the greatest woman in the world next to Grandma, God rest her soul," said Tommy. "I'm calling to tell you that I met a guy on the ship that says he knows you. His name is Henry Viper. He says that you two used to work together for his uncle Johnny Viper back in the day. He even says that he remembers Grandma, especially because of how beautiful she was in her blue dress with her sapphire necklace. He bought me some drinks, Grandpa, and tomorrow I'm meeting him again onshore in Aruba at noon for lunch at Passions on the Beach to introduce him to Sophia." About what seemed like a minute of silence transpired before Tommy said, "Grandpa, are you still there? Can you hear me?"

Frankie finally said, "Tommy, don't do that. Don't meet him again. Don't take Sophia to meet him. I can't tell you why, but that man is nothing but bad news. Don't go near him. That's an order!"

Tommy was shocked by his grandfather's words but did not question him. Growing up in Collinwood and Murray Hill had taught Tommy many things. The most important thing was to never question your family. Tommy's childhood and his love of *The Godfather* movies, parts of which were filmed in Murray Hill, had taught him the value of family, of loyalty to one's family, and now he sensed that this meeting with Henry was going to lead to mayhem.

As Frankie hung up the phone, he took a deep breath, gathered his wits about him, and called an old friend of his who retired in Aruba. Frankie had a lot of friends all over the Caribbean. It was a great place for business.

"Pauly, I have a job for you," said Frankie.

*****

Henry Viper and Frankie Torino had driven cars, run numbers, served as bouncers, and secured girls for Uncle Johnny during their days on Murray Hill. As they entered their twenties, they each felt they deserved a promotion in the rackets that Henry's uncle was running. Johnny was looking for someone to become a lieutenant whose job was to ensure that the police and city councilmen were being paid off to ignore the businesses that he was operating. It took guts, forcefulness, tact, negotiating skills, and a lot of balls to do this job, but it was the key position in the organization if the boss wanted to succeed. Both Henry and Frankie thought they deserved to be the lieutenant. When Uncle Johnny chose Frankie for the job at Frankie's thirtieth birthday party, Henry was devastated. His anger was directed not only at his uncle but at Frankie as well. Thoughts filled him with rage that ran through his brain. He deserved the job. He was family. He deserved the respect from Uncle Johnny that Henry had always shown to him. He figured he was better than Frankie. What had Frankie ever done that Henry couldn't do better? Henry had never learned how to control his anger. It had been a problem forever. He had to bring this to a head. The solution was easy. He decided to go to Frankie's house and settle this man-to-man.

Frankie's house was a small brick bungalow, tidy, but certainly modest. It was in a rural area of Mayfield Heights and was isolated from other homes, thus making it as secure as any fortress in the Cleveland area. Frankie hoped to build a bigger home very soon, and his promotion would certainly hasten the process. Henry was greeted at the door by Camilla, Frankie's wife.

"It's great to see you again, Henry," said Camilla. "I assume that you want to talk to Frankie, but he's not here. Can I help you?"

Henry glared at Camilla. He didn't expect to see her. Although she was oblivious to the goings-on of Frankie's business interests, she knew that Henry and her husband were rivals in Johnny's empire. Sure, they were on the same side most of the time, but they also wanted the glory and prestige that came with being one of Johnny's closest disciples. Henry began to stare at Camilla. His animosity toward Frankie could be dealt with in another way, he said to himself, and what the hell, old habits are hard to break.

Camilla was startled as Henry's glare intensified. She was looking stunning in her strapless, low-cut blue dress, which was accentuated with a beautiful sapphire necklace. Henry noticed her bountiful figure, her beautiful blue eyes that were the exact same color as her necklace, and her gorgeous legs, which were shown off by the short hem on the dress. His attack caught her totally off guard. He came at her even harder than he had attacked Michelle, Ron's mother, and the many other sluts and whores who he had brutalized in his life. And he enjoyed every minute of it. He enjoyed each thrust as he gripped her throat. He enjoyed the panicked look on her face, and most of all, he enjoyed it when she died. As a souvenir, he took the sapphire necklace from her neck. Everybody deserved a trophy after a job well done!

As Henry left Frankie's house, he was smiling. There's no better way to even the score with Frankie than to rape and kill his wife, he thought. The murder part just happened. It was an accident. It was never his intent to do that, but she was screaming so much that he had no choice. And now he felt like he had not only evened the score but had perhaps taken the lead in his battle with Frankie. Driving away, Henry fully expected that someday Frankie might suspect him in Camilla's death. That could be a problem, but what the hell, he would deal with that when it happened. He'd been in the house many times, so even if he hadn't wiped off all his fingerprints before he left, the existence of his prints would be considered normal. He knew there were no witnesses, so he began to think that he got away with murder.

Fifteen minutes after Henry left, Frankie pulled into his drive-way. He was singing *Happy Birthday* as he found Camilla's lifeless body lying in the foyer. Her blue dress and the sapphire necklace had been the presents that Frankie had given to her that morning for her birthday, which they were celebrating that night. She never wore blue dresses, as she thought it was not her color. She'd called Frankie earlier to tell him that she was going to wear both for her birthday dinner. He noticed immediately that the necklace was gone. He shrieked. He cried.

He screamed, "Camilla, Camilla, wake up. Tell me what happened. Who did this to you? Please wake up, please wake up."

And then after forty years of no suspects, no satisfaction, and no revenge, Frankie gets a phone call from his grandson, Tommy, who tells him out of the blue that some guy named Henry Viper knew about the blue dress and the necklace. So Frankie decided to even the score and made that phone call to Aruba.

*****

On the morning that Jake, Bruce, Barbara, Danielle, and Ron planned to kill Henry Viper, they had breakfast together at one of the Central Park restaurants on the ship. They felt that they deserved some red-carpet service, not a buffet, just in case it was their last breakfast together. They verified their plan and knew that Henry would be joining them for dinner at the 7:30 seating at Chops, the best steak house on the ship. As they nervously wondered how they would get through the day, they decided to go ashore to see the wonders of Aruba. They had to do something to fill what could be their final day of freedom if things didn't go as planned.

Chapter 15

Being a hit man for Frankie Torino was a job that afforded Pauly Palmetto a luxurious life that he never could have imagined. He traveled the world. He ate in the best restaurants. He wore the best Italian suits. He drove the newest cars, and he screwed women who were classy in public and whorish in bed. He loved his life. When his cell phone rang, he was at his digs at the Aruba Bubali Luxury Apartments. When Pauly saw that the caller was Frankie himself, he was excited and anticipated another assignment from his boss.

"Hey, Frankie, what's up? It's been a long time!" exalted Pauly as he picked up the phone.

"Hey, Pauly," said Frankie. "How's it hangin'? How you doing with all those gorgeous Dutch women? You gettin' into their shoes?" joked Frankie as they both laughed.

"Look, Pauly," said Frankie as his tone got profoundly serious. "I've got a wet job for you, and it has got to be done tomorrow before that cruise ship *Allure* leaves the port."

Knowing that to Frankie a wet job meant someone was going to die, Pauly said, "Sure, Frankie, whatever you want. That's why you pay me the big bucks. Who's the target?"

Frankie's voice took on an almost-menacing timber, "His name is Henry Viper. He's that big car dealer in Cleveland. He needs to die. He needs to be eliminated to make my world a better place."

"I think I know that guy. Is he the one that's from the West Side who does all those stupid car commercials with that sexy broad, Evangeline?" asked Pauly.

"The very one," answered Frankie.

"Boy, I'd love to screw that broad, Frankie. She makes me hard every time I see those commercials," exclaimed Pauly. "Do I need to fly up to Cleveland to do the job?"

Frankie continued, "No, listen to me. Look, my grandson is on a cruise ship that's docked in Aruba right now. Tommy will be taking Henry to lunch tomorrow about noon at Passions on the Beach. Tommy knows nothing about this and will have his new bride with him. Make it a clean hit and make sure that he and his wife are nowhere near Henry when you make your move. Make this happen! Maybe use one of the disguises. I love that fake full beard you sometimes wore back in the day. Maybe get him before he even walks into the joint. That should make it easier for your getaway," continued Frankie. "And, Pauly, to show you how much I respect you, I'm doubling your normal fee this time because this is personal for me. I know that you'll do it right. I believe in you. Hell, maybe you'll be able to afford to buy that beach house in Jamaica as a second home you've always talked about. I'll e-mail a picture of Henry just to ensure you recognize the asshole."

Both men roared out loud as the deal was sealed.

"And finally, Pauly, as you pull the trigger, you might want to tell Henry that I never got to see Camilla in that blue dress and sapphire necklace!"

After he hung up with Pauly, Frankie called his grandson.

"Hey, Tommy, I've been thinking. I was wrong to tell you not to see Henry Viper again. That was stupid on my part. Henry and I go way back, and of course, I've had some battles with him, but overall, he's a nice goombah, and he is a part of our Cleveland family. I respect that. I respect how he's turned his life around. Why not take Sophia and meet him for lunch tomorrow and send him my best? Catch him up on the neighborhood and give him my blessing. I'll appreciate that a lot. Funny that you said you were meeting him at Passions on the Beach. Your dad and I have been there many times.

I'll call the owner and set up a private table for noon. Just tell them I sent you," said Frankie as convincingly as he could.

"Of course, Grandpa, you know I'll do whatever you want."

*****

After breakfast, Jake and his coconspirators put on their hiking shoes so they could explore the island of Aruba. One side is a tropical paradise, the other a desert. They needed a distraction as they tried to avoid thinking about what they were going to do to Henry during dinner. They rented scooters and rode on every road possible even though their minds were elsewhere, causing Jake and Danielle to drive off the road a few times. It seemed like the group was purposely trying to get lost. They spent three hours inside the Quadirikiri Cave. They visited the Bushiribana Ruins, the Alto Vista Chapel, and even toured the California Lighthouse; but despite all the wonderful attractions, their nerves were getting the best of them.

Tommy and Sophia got to Passions on the Beach at about 11:45. Henry was already there as the couple moved to the private room that Frankie had arranged.

"Aah, you must be Sophia, and yes, my dear, you are as beautiful as Tommy said. Damn, I wish I could be twenty-five again," said Henry, using the same lines that he'd used all his life. Sophia, dressed in short shorts and a low-cut blouse that exposed her youthful breasts, blushed as Henry kissed her hand.

"Tommy, tell your grandpa how much I've always appreciated what he did for me over the years and how much I admired what he did in Murray Hill. He and my uncle Johnny built that neighborhood. They helped people. They set the tone for what is good and right in this world and eliminated problems that sometimes fucked things up. They supported the church. They made the businesses profitable, and who knows, but I wouldn't be surprised at all if someday Murray Hill builds statues in their honor. Hell, they should put them right there in the park!" continued Henry while Tommy and Sophia smiled at every word.

"Henry, my grandpa told me that you really were a great guy," said Tommy enthusiastically just as Pauly Palmetto entered the room.

Pauly was wearing a long-frocked coat, much too warm for the tropical climate, a black baseball cap, and a full fake beard that almost covered his eyes. His own mother would not have recognized him.

DON'T TELL A SOUL

"What the fuck?" said Henry. "Who are you? Get the fuck away from us. Leave the kids alone," pleaded Henry, sensing what was about to happen as he saw Pauly's gun dressed in a silencer.

As Pauly readied himself to put the six rounds into the head and torso of Henry Viper, he calmly said, "You know, Henry, Frankie agrees with you. Camilla really would have looked great wearing that blue dress and sapphire necklace." And then Pauly calmly emptied his gun.

After pulling the trigger, Pauly slowly retreated through the back door and walked away before Tommy and Sophia could get over the shock of what they had just witnessed. Pauly had done it again.

The Aruba police force arrived about ten minutes after the shots were fired. Tommy ran for help into the main part of the restaurant as he was cleaning up the vomit that was pouring out of Sophia's mouth, causing her to choke uncontrollably. This gave Pauly even more time to slowly walk away from suspicion, stuffing his disguise in the nearest garbage bin. The reputation of the Aruba police force was still shaky after the famous Natalie Holloway disappearance, where it appeared that the cops were protecting Joran van der Sloot because he was a rich, connected kid with prominent parents. There were rarely any murders in Aruba, and even the veteran cops panicked when they had one to investigate.

"Did either of you get a good look at the guy?" asked Detective Luuk Sylvan, a twenty-five-year veteran of the police force. He had intense grey eyes that peered at Tommy, looking for any sign of lies.

"He was tall, wore a black hat, a black coat, and had a full beard," answered Tommy.

Sophia nodded in agreement.

"Did he say anything before he pulled the trigger?" asked Sylvan.

Tommy was quick to answer.

As he squeezed Sophia's arm tightly, he said, "No, he didn't say a word. Just pulled the trigger! Scared the shit out of us!"

Sophia looked at Tommy and understood immediately that she wasn't supposed to tell a soul what the killer had said.

After another hour of questions that got the Aruban police nowhere, Tommy and Sophia were released to return to the *Allure*. Detective Sylvan thanked them for their help, got their contact information, and admitted that he had no reason to hold them or charge them with any wrongdoing. As Henry's body was being taken from the restaurant, Jake, Barb, Bruce, Ron, and Danielle were stopped on their scooters by the blockades set up by the police to secure the crime scene. Hundreds of people, mainly tourists from the *Allure*, had gathered in front of the restaurant.

"I wonder what happened here," Jake said to no one in particular.

"It must have been pretty bad," said Danielle. "You rarely see this number of cop cars even in LA."

Ron joked, "Hell, I have when they were after my ass!"

The levity was especially appreciated by Bruce whose cold feet had now turned to ice.

As the body was put into the ambulance, Jake heard someone yell out, "Hey, the victim was some big-time Cleveland car dealer. He was on the *Allure* with us. Looks like he was bumped off by a guy with a silencer. That's why nobody heard the shots. Lucky for his friends that the killer didn't get them too. I think his name was Henry!"

When Jake heard these words, his face became pale. His heart thumped erratically, and his stomach churned like he was about to vomit. He was in total shock at this turn of events. As Jake looked at his friends, his first comment was, "Son of a bitch, God does work in strange ways."

At dinner that night, the table at Chops was minus one person, Henry Viper. It was a formal night on the ship, so Jake, Barb, Bruce,

Danielle, and Ron were dressed in the finest suits and dresses. The meal included the best surf and turf of the cruise and the most-expensive wine and champagne.

Their private room was in the far back of the restaurant, enabling them to talk openly about what had just happened. Ron was the first to speak after all of them were seated. As he spoke, he stared directly at Danielle.

"Looking at you, Danielle, in your great dress and seeing all of you in your splendor, I now understand what I missed by not going to the prom so long ago. God, that was a terrible mistake, and Danielle, I am sorry."

Ron's apology was accompanied by a sheepish smile. Danielle returned his smile with a glow that devoured Ron completely, and then they all admitted to each other that they looked damn good for folks in their early seventies.

As the salads came, Barb told them how to properly dispose of the ricin that they all possessed.

"Open the container and flush the powder down the toilet in one of the public bathrooms. Don't flush it down the toilet in your own room in case that flush fails to dispose of it. Rinse the container and throw it into the restroom garbage can. Be sure the ricin doesn't touch your hands and wash your hands thoroughly," she strongly advised. "The stuff will eventually go into the ocean and never be found."

They all agreed to comply and thanked Barb for her medical wisdom.

As the drinks continued to flow on the last formal dinner of the cruise, Jake asked all of them if they could have gone through with it. Could they really have poisoned Henry Viper? Danielle admitted that she had second thoughts from the beginning.

"God, guys, I'm still a hippie. I paint weird paintings. I believe in peace and love, not war. I live in a wacky place called Los Angeles. But you know what? I might have been able to go through with it. I loved Michelle, but I'm just not positive how I may have acted. I just don't know."

Bruce said, "Jake, I liked Michelle a lot, but you loved her. I was here mainly to support you, and I admit that I got caught up into the mob mentality of all of this. So I agree with Danielle. I think I might have done it, but I really don't know. Probably not. When I was a kid, I always used to think that if a burglar ever broke into my house, I would fight him. I imagined that I would hit him with my fists and my baseball bat. But you know what? I doubt if I would have done anything other than piss my pants while I hid under the bed."

Everybody laughed as Bruce's words, combined with the alcohol, was easing the tension of the day and calming their collective nerves.

"You know what, Jake?" Ron asked. "I think I would have thrown the poison into Henry's asparagus, knowing that nobody ever eats asparagus. So I would have done my part but would have believed in my heart that somebody else, not me, really poisoned him. Remember, guys, I am a totally reformed man!" He was staring at Danielle as he said those words.

It was Barb's turn to talk, "Guys, remember I came up with the idea. I created the poison. I gave the idea to Jake. I told you how to commit the perfect crime, so I think I did my part. I loved Michelle probably more than anyone here other than Jake, and yes, I had second thoughts. I'm a doctor. I'm supposed to save lives. I have no idea if I could have poisoned him tonight, but I still would've had tons of guilt if any of us had given him the ricin and succeeded in killing him. I'm glad that we didn't have to do it," Barb admitted.

Finally, it was time for Jake to speak. His sincerity was obvious.

"You all know this already, but I loved Michelle ever since the day at Baker when she asked me to dance. Maybe it was puppy love at first, but it grew way beyond that over the next six years. As I said at her funeral, she was my soul mate, my best friend, and someone who always brought out the best in me. When she first started to pull away from me, I thought that I'd done something to hurt her. That was hard to live with, but when Barb told me what really happened, I had to find the man who destroyed her life and mine. At that point, my life changed. I had to admit the truth to myself, and that was that I needed to get revenge while being fully aware that doing so might cost me my family and my career. I had already lost Sarah. All I focused on was revenge for the rapist that caused Michelle to eventually commit suicide. She deserved that. She deserved my understanding. If she had only confided in me! All I could do then was to find that vile felon. I had to even the score. And to fulfill that wish of making things right, I turned to all of you, the best friends that a guy could ever have. My thanks to all of you. I'll never forget what you were willing to do, but let's agree right now that we'll never tell a soul what we almost did." Tears filled everyone's eyes as Jake raised his glass and said, "To Michelle!"

When the *Allure* arrived in Fort Lauderdale, the group left the ship together. Disembarking the ship was easy. The scuttlebutt in the departure lines was all about Henry and why he was killed. Tommy continued to say nothing to Sophia as she began to understand the family business. Pauly was back at his condo in Aruba, wondering what woman he would screw today and when his boss would give him another problem to solve. Frankie appreciated Pauly's phone call, indicating that he had succeeded again, and began to cry as he thought about the beautiful blue dress and sapphire necklace that his beloved wife never got to fully enjoy.

Jake, Barb, Danielle, Bruce, and Ron decided to ride back to the airport together and commissioned the first minivan available at the Port Everglades.

"To the airport, sir," Jake said after everyone boarded the van. "Don't call me, sir," said the driver. "My name is Bill Butler. A lot of my friends call me Mr. Vermont. Welcome back to Florida. I hope you had a great cruise."

"Thanks, Bill," said Bruce.

"It was the best," said Jake.

"We'll never forget it," added Barb.

"Ah, Vermont," said Ron, "the land of snowballs, Bernie Sanders, and Ethan Allen."

Bill laughed as Danielle added, "And all sorts of hippie, weirdo freaks."

Bruce paid Bill when they reached the Fort Lauderdale International Airport and tipped him well. He turned to the others and saw that Danielle had grabbed Ron's hand and that Jake had grabbed Barb's.

Bruce smiled as he saw two new budding romances and laughed as he looked at them and said, "Now, guys, don't forget. Don't tell a soul!"

About The Auhor

Jim Wasowski, a native of Indiana, taught history and coached basketball for the Cleveland public schools for thirty-one years. He
also taught history and historical research at Edison State College
in Florida for seven years. He has coauthored five books on how to
teach history. This is his first novel. He lives in Southwest Florida
and currently enjoys his life as Mr. Trivia of Southwest Florida, having written and produced over 1,800 live games.

Connie Romoser Friess was born in Ohio and worked in the
computer industry for over forty years, including ten years as a tech-
nical analyst for ADP. She teaches local fitness classes in Southwest
Florida and has spent her whole life as an avid reader. This is also her
first novel.

Jim and his coauthor, Connie, have been married for three years
and enjoy travelling and playing golf.

CPSIA information can be obtained
at www.ICGtesting.com
Printed in the USA
LVHW010155100221
678885LV00003B/417